LOST VENGEANCE

The past for Lomas, alias Ilyich Palatnik, a Russian emigré living in England, looms out of the normality of a London street, when he finds himself on the track of the penal camp killer of his mother. With revenge in his heart Lomas tracks ex-Major Igor Kunetsov to his home in the far east of the Soviet Union, but there the Major's daughter, Inga, produces a counter-emotion. The deed of vengeance concluded Lomas flees westward with Inga, closely pursued not only by the police, but also by the KGB.

Lost Vengeance

by

Christopher Portway

Dales Large Print Books
Long Preston, North Yorkshire,
BD23 4ND, England.

British Library Cataloguing in Publication Data.

Portway, Christopher
    Lost vengeance.

    A catalogue record of this book is
    available from the British Library

    ISBN   1-84262-343-5 pbk

First published in Great Britain in 1973
by Robert Hale & Company

Copyright © Robert Hale & Company 1973

The moral right of the author has been asserted

Published in Large Print 2004 by arrangement with
Robert Hale Ltd.

Dales Large Print is an imprint of Library Magna Books Ltd.

Printed and bound in Great Britain by
T.J. (International) Ltd., Cornwall, PL28 8RW

For aeronautical advice the author is indebted to Bruce Maclellan and Paul Cermak as he is likewise to TomWright for a contribution of a less specialized nature. To the author's wife, Anna, goes gratitude for checking the script.

CHAPTER ONE

Lomas was staring into the shop window, seeing nothing. Not even his own reflection, hunched and despondent, caught his eye. Behind him a broken skein of traffic snarled but made no impact.

It was Sunday, and Lomas hated Sundays. An early riser all the week, he was unable to break the habit on Sundays. And Sundays were a vacuum. Even the pubs stayed shut till midday.

The mean streets behind Waterloo Station where Lomas lived in a two-room tenement invariably drove him across the river on Sunday mornings. At least the Strand offered an illusion of a purpose in life that his weekday job in a city travel agency failed to give him. Not that the job was a bad one. The pay was reasonable and he even liked it. But there were too many anti-climaxes. He could fill a client and himself full of enthusiasm for a holiday sunspot of exotic allure, make all the arrangements with ruthless, almost personal, intensity, and only the client would go. Lomas knew a bit about the world into the bargain, though his knowledge was of parts few holiday-makers cared to visit.

The trigger in Lomas's mind switched it to the well-worn canvas of his life. When bored and at a loose end, he would invariably look back; never forward. The past held a picture of morbid interest that grew more colourful with age. The future stayed grey.

Prison. The screen always came to life with the prison. He could never get a clear picture of anything earlier. Occasionally, the thin sheen of his Ukraine home flickered for an instant to detonate glimpses of the little wooden school in Kiev, the larch avenue outside his house and the bank leading down to the Dneiper river where he used to play. But even the glimpses were vague and distant, like looking through the wrong end of a telescope. The prison on the other hand came through bright and clear, its harsh lines etched deep. It had all begun a week before his sixteenth birthday and the date – 16th August 1945 – had become the first milestone of his life.

It was a common enough story in the Ukraine. Nationalism had always swelled to dangerous proportions in this region of the

USSR. It was in fact the very elixir of its people, a quintessence to dilute the horror of the ruthless imposition of collectivization upon them. With the German invasion of their land came the chance to shoulder off the yoke of Soviet oppression. Thousands took it and welcomed the Nazi invaders as the liberators they could have been. But the Ukranians had reckoned without the German mentality and the warped streak of cruelty that runs through the Teutonic race. As Soviet oppression became Nazi oppression, so Ukranian resistance hardened, and upon the blood-soaked plains around Kiev its soldiers rallied and fought with a courage that was terrible to behold.

Within weeks of the ending of the war the Soviet Government of Joseph Stalin acknowledged its debts and took its retribution. A few impersonal war memorials settled the former, but for the initial indiscretions the price was without parallel in mankind's catalogue of human suffering. Hundreds of thousands of Ukranians; whole families, whole generations, were herded, in unspeakable conditions, to the prison camps of eastern Russia, there to serve their sentences in servitude.

Lomas had been one of the unfortunates.

Together with his mother, he had ended up at camp nine in Mordovia. Though barely sixteen, he was deemed not too young to shoulder a portion of the crimes of his father. And his father's only indiscretion was that of remaining a policeman under German occupation in an effort to alleviate the sufferings of his fellow citizens in Darnitza, now an industrial suburb of Kiev. That he had, by so doing, saved many lives made no impression at his 'trial'. Lomas's father had clicked for 25 years – a 'quarter' in the parlance of the camps – and was despatched to Karaganda. Lomas himself got six years by reason, as they put, of 'aiding and comforting a traitor'. But his mother's sentence, though no longer than his own, erupted into the most savage of all. Its execution – and, incidentally, her own – made the second milestone of his life and one that left a scar across his soul.

It had happened at the Potma transit camp. The whole of South-west Mordovia is a place of exile; a land of barbed wire, watch-towers and despair. And it is at Potma that a new inmate will receive his initiation into the twilight world.

The batch of male and female prisoners,

still individualistic in their personal garb, had shuffled into the administrative square for counting and allocation to different compounds. From the nearest watch-tower a bored soldier leaned against the parapet nursing a carbine, his forage cap pushed to the back of his head. Other soldiers chivvied and slapped their charges, only flustering them and adding to their general nervousness and apprehension. Rows of wooden huts, depressing in their symmetry, offered the only feature upon a flat wilderness of sandy scrub.

An officer in a greatcoat, accompanied by his retinue, stood before the new arrivals. In a toneless voice he recited the simple instructions that went for a welcome to Potma. He spoke in Russian though realizing that, with all the groups that went before and with all those that were to come, there were present a dozen nationalities each with their own tongues and customs. The short speech ended, the group broke into excited chatter as translations passed along the ranks. One of the few to remain silent was Lomas. He had understood the meaning of the speech and turned to his mother to smile encouragement at what would soon be the parting of the ways.

His mother had understood, too, but the implications took longer to permeate the old and frightened mind. Maybe fatigue and hunger had confused her senses, for she must have guessed her destination to be different to that of her son by virtue of her sex. Lomas became aware of her startled eyes; the sudden collapse of the lined face.

Without warning, the old woman had left the column and was running wildly towards the gate. Lomas promptly set out in pursuit but was forcibly restrained by two guards. While he was struggling, he heard the single shot from the direction of the tower and glimpsed the soldier lowering his weapon. Before madness overtook him and he was knocked unconscious by a blow, the sight of his mother, still running but dragging a useless leg like a wounded hare, was for ever imprinted upon his mind. Not even had they allowed her the privilege of a warning shot.

It took Lomas several days to piece together the rest of the story. The shot had brought the cons* running to the wire, but the living compounds were some distance from the administration block. Their stories varied as hate expanded the facts; their methods of

*Colloquialism for convicts

telling were either wrapped in foul obscenities or gentle detraction from the truth, depending upon whether or not the teller was aware of Lomas's relationship to the victim.

A hospital orderly – a 'trusty' – who was leaving the medical block at the time of the incident probably gave the most accurate version of the subsequent occurrences. He was a Latvian, a timid little man trying to appease both his fellow cons and authority and consequently was despised by both. Lomas nagged him unmercifully for every detail.

In the neighbouring square, wired but out of bounds to cons, his mother, moaning softly, had staggered towards the fence. The Major and two junior officers, not even bothering to run, followed. Out of sight of the new batch of prisoners as well as those attracted by the shot, they slowed to watch the woman make her pathetic efforts to climb the wire. A soldier in another watchtower started to shout the standard warning but was silenced by the Major's gesture.

His victim, with superhuman effort, managed to ascend three-quarters of the way, fighting off each barbed strand that plucked at bulbous sleeves and skirt. Then she ceased fighting to become abruptly calm as if aware of her dignity. She turned her head to face the trio below.

Drawing his pistol, the Major looked into the proud eyes and shot her three times.

The body jerked, straightened and fell forward through the wire, there to hang head down, a grotesque doll, its garments parting to reveal thin white legs.

The Major reholstered his pistol but made no move. He appeared to be enjoying the pitiful sight before him. He murmured 'shot while attempting to escape' as if to convince both himself and his colleagues of the correctness of his action. Two soldiers were summoned to remove the remains from the wire.

That she was dead was virtually certain, but what happened next injected into Lomas the last basic ingredient of hate. With difficulty the body was loosened from the barbs to drop with a sickening thud to the ground close by the Major. He circled the corpse curiously. A look of loathing contorted his face. With an intake of breath he viciously kicked at the chest, stoving in the ribs. Unsatisfied, he repeated the action to the head, only desisting when he saw the mess on his shoes.

The Latvian said one of the soldiers that had removed the body was sick.

The Major's name was Igor Kunetsov,

KGB.* Major Igor Kunetsov.

Lomas would never forget the tale the Latvian had told him. Nor the name of his mother's executioner. In his heart he also harboured an awareness that, even were it possible, he hadn't the guts to do anything about it.

It was seldom that Lomas allowed himself to dwell upon his mother's death. Usually he shied away from the subject, pushing it to the back of his mind. To help he had even made up a set of excuses to cover the incident. His mother, after all, had crossed into a shooting zone. The Major himself had been brutalized by a brute of a regime. The kicking business, revolting though it was, had at least occurred after his mother's death. His subsequent life shone all the brighter from this little enclave of darkness.

Lomas had served six years without remission. He had neither begged for forgiveness nor antagonized his jailers. In 1951, he had been released, and by virtue of a certain skill with boat designing took a job in the shipyards of Murmansk. The following year two events occurred. He learnt of the

*Committee for state security.

death of his father and received the offer of a draughtsman's position at the Soviet naval base at Porkkala, on Finnish territory near Helsinki. His father's demise had no bearing on his acceptance. He would have gone anyway; pleasantly astounded by the fact that his police dossier allowed him a possible stepping-stone to emigration, Lomas was then 22. In 1955 the situation in the Gulf of Finland allowed his countrymen to return Porkkala to the Finns, but Lomas had remained. There had been no dramatic requests for Finnish asylum or heavy denunciation of his Soviet citizenship. He had simply drifted into the local community via a short spell in a refugee camp and from there had drifted, via a Hull cargo vessel, to England. Perhaps 'drifted' had become the operative word in his new life. A series of jobs in Tyneside and Tilbury offered little scope for his designing talents and in London, where anything can happen, it did. It was luck that had given him his travel agency position. He was simply at the right place at the right moment. With a static job he had done his best to conform to the English pattern of life. Going from one extreme to the other, he'd tried his hand at golf but had never felt 'accepted' at the club. Later he had joined an aero club outside London with the purpose of gaining a pilot's licence that had been nearly his in Kiev just before the end of the war. Again he had failed to stay the course. Ballroom dancing had been another project he'd set himself. If he couldn't make it with his fellow-men, maybe he'd cut a more dashing figure with the fair sex. But once more something seemed to be missing – including the fair sex.

Lomas became aware of his own reflection in the shop window. He saw a stark face, stern and lacking the facilities to smile. An expanse of forehead resulted more from a receding hairline than an intellectual ability. The eyes were deep in the head, giving an impression of immense fatigue, even suffering, that he secretly enjoyed. That he carried 'the Slav look' was obvious to anyone so it might as well be the 'tragic Slav look' to the simple, decent, unknowledgeable Londoners with whom he lived. Maybe he played the game too well, for, though everyone was kindly disposed towards him, he could claim few friends. Women showed initial interest only to lose it upon discovering his depth of feeling to fall short of expectation. Anyway, at thirty-seven he was not a catch for every girl along the way.

The traffic snarl had got through to him now and Lomas was back again in the present. In a few minutes it would be midday and he could wander down to the 'Wig and Pen' for a noggin with Tim Faraday. Tim was a member of this most English of establishments as well as being a fellow clerk in the travel office. Lomas hadn't analysed the relationship but he supposed Tim to be one of his closest friends. Funny these English with their 'noggins', but he'd caught the bug. He thought he was beginning to understand what a Britisher would fight to the death for but could never put into words.

He was seeing the window display. High-fidelity and stereophonic equipment in neat, impressive rows with jazzy prices to match. Another but more modern English fad. The greater the number of knobs, muting switches and speakers the better. What came out didn't really matter as long as it was loud. He remembered Russia. There they had no equipment but they did have what came out. He supposed it hadn't changed.

Several passers-by had stopped to gaze at the amplifiers and tape recorders. In the glass, he idly counted three men. Two were youths, dreaming of possession. The third was Major Igor Kunetsov.

CHAPTER TWO

Of course it was a mistake, an optical illusion. His morbid thoughts of a moment ago were playing delayed-action tricks with his eyes. That a piece of his past twenty-two years and seven thousand miles away from a hideous world so utterly alien to an Englishman's life could be standing next to him outside a Strand music shop was ludicrous. Lomas laughed to himself, but the laugh was audible. The two youths glanced at him sharply.

He turned slowly to have a look at the older man. The likeness was extraordinary even taking into consideration those twenty years. The bushy eyebrows were heavier, more in keeping with an ageing face. A mop of unruly grey hair that had once been a striking feature – it had instigated a nickname of 'Steel wool' – was now tamed, submissive and plastered limply over the skull. But the pronounced cheekbones had not changed, nor the fish eyes that seldom blinked. In days gone by, Lomas had likened the eyes to those of a doll, only closing when laid down. The same foolish notion rose unbidden now and it was this more than anything that held his attention. Lomas mentally tried to fit a khaki uniform into the stooping figure in place of the badly cut suit but failed. Only the eyes left little room for doubt.

For a moment the man's gaze passed over Lomas, held for a moment and moved on. There was no recognition.

As he moved away towards Trafalgar Square Lomas fell in behind him. The 'noggin' with Faraday was momentarily forgotten. The pavement was strangely empty after the weekday surge of movement and he was able to keep his quarry in sight from considerable distance. Repeatedly he told himself what a fool he was, but his footsteps were relentless in their new purpose.

How long the inner conflict would have lasted is debatable. In the event the footsteps were triumphant as far as the Strand Palace Hotel. The man entered the mirror-glass portals to pause a moment at the theatre agency in the garish vestibule. It was this pause that allowed Lomas to catch up and hear the demand for the key to room 437. The voice was deep with a foreign inflection.

To Lomas it was Russian.

He allowed the man a couple of minutes then, still hesitant, approached the clerk behind reception.

'Excuse my asking, but could you tell me the name of the occupant of room 437?' Lomas smiled disarmingly adding, 'I saw him go towards the lift and thought I recognised him.'

The clerk consulted a ledger. 'It's a Mr Reprostovich.'

'Can you by any chance tell me what he's doing here in London and how long he's staying?'

'That sort of information we are not allowed to give.'

Lomas turned away, but caught the sly look the clerk gave him. He didn't think he could get away with less than a pound. The clerk's paw slid expertly over the note and he re-examined the book together with a sheaf of registration forms.

'Says here he's with a Soviet Trade Mission from Siberia. Gives a personal address as 38 Lermontov Street, Khabarovsk.' The pronunciation did not make it sound quite like that but Lomas knew where he meant. 'He's here for a week; four days to go.' The pounds-worth was up.

'Nothing more?'

'Nothing more.'

A glint of pale sunshine flashed in the glass panels of the swing doors. It made him jump. A pound the poorer, he made his way back to the 'Wig and Pen'.

The plush maroon seat coverings and permanent dusk of the small bar-room offered warm familiarity to Lomas. He nodded to some of the regulars as he pushed his way through the crush towards Faraday in the far corner.

'You're late, a whole forty minutes late,' said the tall, gangling youth with mock severity.

'Sorry and thanks,' replied Lomas, accepting the proffered pint. He offered no explanation.

Faraday was the opposite of Lomas. Fair hair, boyish open face, old-school tie and voice to match, he had come to regard himself as not only friend but protector of his fellow clerk. Faraday considered himself fitted for greater things than offered by the tasks of the travel agency. That he did not attain them was a source of constant puzzlement to him. To assuage a disappointment and to deflect the brutal truth he took it upon himself to act as father-confessor to the friendless and tragic Lomas. His influence over him gave Faraday the self-assurance he lacked in more profitable fields.

Before the couple had sunk the first pint Faraday became aware that his protégé was absorbed in other matters. The fact worried him. Maybe he was losing his grip. Perplexed, Faraday watched as Lomas swirled the remains of the beer in his tankard.

'What's biting you, old son?'

Lomas looked up and smiled his sad smile. It was sadder than usual.

'It's nothing,' he said, knowing he would have to tell Faraday. The chap would bludgeon it out of him anyway.

'If it's a problem, two minds are better than one.'

Lomas turned to his companion. There seemed no reason not to tell him.

'A bit of my past caught up with me today. At least, it might just conceivably have done.'

Faraday was all ears. A satisfied concern spread across the open face. His responsibilities were not to be spurned.

The hubbub of the bar seemed to die as Lomas told of the events of the morning. Translated into words, they sounded the more fatuous.

Into the vacuum of his revelations the hubbub gushed. A painted doll of a woman laughed piercingly. Tobacco smoke turned blue as it floated to be the ceiling.

But Faraday didn't laugh. Lomas wished he had. It might have washed the incident out of his system. Instead Faraday said, 'Since your Ruskie friend's here for a few more days, perhaps we can find out more about him.'

Lomas drained his glass. 'And what if he *is* the man?' Faraday made no immediate reply. He knew that Lomas was relying upon him again. To cover his indecision he ordered two more beers even though it was not his round. Possibly it was only the beer talking when at length he replied: 'Had it been my mother, I'd kill him.'

The words had seemed harmless enough to Faraday at the time. After all, Lomas had first to prove his case. Even this was going to be next to impossible. The whole thing was farcical. Only it wasn't funny. Lomas had let the thing go in deep and was brooding on it. The ill-considered advice he'd given him that Sunday in the pub was obviously not the root of the trouble. It did appear, however, to have confirmed something in the back of the chap's mind. They'd both gone to the hotel the next day and after a lot of hanging around they'd seen the man. To Faraday he'd looked innocuous enough. But with Lomas the sight of him had stoked a passion, an inner conflict even. On the Thursday Lomas had taken the whole day off. He'd rung the manager to report a sore throat. Faraday knew what he was going to do and hoped it would be the end of the affair. Perhaps they could then get back to normality in their relationship. He wondered why he'd become so attached to one so different and a Ruski of all people. The trouble was they took life so seriously, so dramatically. All those passions, conflicts and torments. Thank heavens he himself was just a sane ordinary Englishman.

It never occurred to Faraday that, in fact, he was not so different to Lomas after all.

Lomas was back in the hotel. He had been there since six that morning. The night staff had given him some odd looks but had become accustomed to his presence on one of the hard-backed chairs near the revolving doors.

Lomas had come to a decision. Somehow

he would get to the bottom of the business today. If necessary, he would confront Reprostovich as he stepped out of the lift. Ask him point blank who he was. But here Lomas's decision began to show ragged edges. Surprise was the key and there might not be the opportunity for surprise. If Reprostovich *was* Kunetsov he'd have years of practice in hiding his real identity. And *if* it was Kunetsov, then Lomas had no wish for his own identity to be known in advance. In advance of what? Lomas asked himself this question for the umpteenth time and came up with a confusion of doubts, hopes and dreads. It was no good being rational. First catch your hare, as the British say. It was Reprostovich's last day in London. If he was *not* Kunetsov, then Lomas could return to the routine of normal life and forget the whole incident. *That* was a more realistic approach; a more rational outlook. He began to beseech Comrade Reprostovich to remain Comrade Reprostovich.

The day staff came on duty and Lomas recognized the reception clerk. The man likewise recognized him and gave an icy nod. Lomas supposed the night clerk had volunteered they had a 'queer' in the vestibule. He didn't care. A couple of cleaning women started vacuuming the carpets, pointedly stabbing his legs with the suction head. One wore a sort of woollen cap comforter with folded-in ear muffs. Lomas remembered the forage caps they wore at Potma.

Guests were emerging from the lifts for breakfast. Lomas began a game with himself, estimating which floor they were on from the duration of the motor's whine. But people began stopping it at different floors and so spoilt the game. He was calculating the average number of stops per hour when Reprostovich appeared. Unused to the ways of foreign hotels, he was carrying a heavy grip himself.

Lomas watched him move into the hall, deposit his bag with the hall porter and enter the restaurant. As he walked Lomas searched in vain for some mannerism, a tiny movement that would reveal the man for what he was. It was the same over breakfast. Lomas chose a table some distance away but one that offered frontal surveillance. Reprostovich had poached eggs and numerous cups of coffee but gave not the slightest hint of being Kunetsov. Lomas tried building up the younger face he remembered into the older one now before him. He listened, straining his ears, to catch the sound of the voice as Reprostovich gave his breakfast order and room number. But nothing clicked.

The meal came to an end for Lomas before he could get to his toast. Conscious of the fact that his last chance was ebbing away, he watched the older man go. Uncertain what to do, he followed, leaving a pound note in his saucer. He passed Reprostovich paying his account at the reception desk. Lomas heard him ask about ways and means of getting to Kensington Air Terminal. At least the chance was being prolonged.

At the booking agency kiosk Lomas paused, pretending to be interested in the theatre posters. Out of the corner of his eye he saw Reprostovich, bag in hand, making for the street.

On impulse Lomas strode to the revolving doors, arriving as the other was having difficulty with his grip. Lomas smiled, good naturedly holding the doors so that Reprostovich and his load could pass through.

Lomas spoke five words. They were in Russian and were obscene. They were words known to all who were at Potma. He spoke quietly as if ashamed to use them.

Had not Reprostovich been occupied with his grip he might have weathered the shock.

Just for an instant, a fleeting moment of time, the mask slipped. The eyes that locked upon Lomas were those of Kunetsov and in them the years fell away.

A second later Reprostovich was smiling his thanks as the revolving doors ushered him gently into a crowded Strand.

Lomas remained in the hotel. There seemed no reason to go to Kensington Air Terminal.

The ensuing months brought no peace to Lomas. The fact that he had satisfied himself that Reprostovich was his mother's killer offered no solution. Instead it offered another and far larger problem. Recollections of camp life, fragments of forgotten incidents and the nightmare of the murder added to the turmoil of his mind. It affected his work, Faraday started avoiding him and even his health began to suffer.

That Reprostovich, or Kunetsov, had become a deep-rooted obsession with Lomas was obvious even to him. To get rid of the obsession was the problem. He tried to persuade himself that the momentary lapse on Kunetsov's part in the revolving doors of the Strand Palace was imagination, a piece of wishful thinking conjured up to give the earlier affair a tidy ending. But it was no good. Lomas *knew* it was Kunetsov. It was an issue that could not be avoided.

So what? What could he do about it? The questions hammered at his brain day and night. He knew he had to see Kunetsov again. There developed a sort of love-hate relationship between him and the man who had committed the crime against a gentle old woman that Lomas could barely remember. The idea of going to Khabarovsk had been born the moment he had learnt that Kunetsov lived there. Now the idea was part of the obsession. But what would he do when he got there? This was a question with no answer. High-sounding phrases like ensuring justice was done circled and drained from the plug-hole of his mind. He'd get no help from the Soviet authorities. He could even be in trouble himself on that score for, in spite of his British citizenship, the Soviets were hardly likely to love an emigrant. And one with a camp record at that. It began nagging at Lomas that he might have done something before Kunetsov had left London. But the British police, for very different reasons, would not have wanted to interfere either. After all, the crime took place in another country, it occurred more than twenty-five years ago and there was no proof. No, this bringing to justice would have to be a personal affair.

Things were brought to a head when Lomas lost his job. It came as no surprise to him. Twice he had been warned by the manager that his work had deteriorated. To Lomas it was but another score to settle with Kunetsov. Faraday pretended to be desolated but his acting was bad. There were suddenly no ties.

Lomas had considerable savings in the bank. The formalities of obtaining a Soviet tourist visa were tedious, but not difficult. By mid-September he was ready to go.

What he intended to do in Khabarovsk Lomas really had not the slightest idea. He took it as an omen, however, that, exactly a year to the day after the unmasking, he was following Kunetsov to, if need be, the end of the earth.

CHAPTER THREE

The city of Khabarovsk sprawls lethargically alongside the great River Amur. It flexes concrete muscles; stretches limbs of bricks and mortar, giving an impression of a metropolis overshadowing a turgid stream. The Amur, three miles wide, ignores these antics, flowing disdainfully by to its reunion with the Ussuri there, to become a mighty sheet of water reflecting the distant blue hills of China. And Khabarovsk pretends not to notice.

Standing respectfully back from the pretentious fountains, the blood-red carnation beds and the gunmetal Lenin, arm outstretched on his granite dais, hovers the Dolny Vostok Hotel. It melts into a façade of grandiose aspirations but limited means that circle Karl Marx Square. Across one of the approach roads a crimson banner shouts death to imperialist warmongers, the output tonnage of the Amur Cable Works and how happy the Soviet people are.

The Dolny Vostok is a typical Intourist-run hotel. It is graded first class, this means only that you pay more for its services. The one service it did offer, Lomas had quite a job to avoid. He did not, on any account, require a guide to pad with him round the town.

Lomas had arrived in Khabarovsk that morning. The big TU-114 turboprop had tipped him out on to an airport crisp under a late September sun. The journey had been an anti-climax. A single night in an excruciating Moscow hotel and on again across the vast world of Siberia. He was astounded what twenty years could do to a man. Here he was in the land of his birth, yet he felt a complete stranger. It was odd, but he resented the patronizing manner which he, a tourist, was afforded. Lomas had abruptly felt the cold loneliness of a man with no country. England was his home all right, make no mistake, but he could not shake off the fact it was a home by act of clemency, not by right. His passport offered the protection of a British government, but he wondered how far that protection spread to the likes of him. Someone had told him it was unwise to return to Soviet territory, that the MVD* had long memories (as if he

*Branch of Soviet Intelligence responsible for prisons, immigration, police and fire services.

34

didn't know) but the doubts had not been strong enough to deflect him from his mission. After all, there had been no dual-nationality nonsense and he'd even served his sentence for the one 'debt' his former country had chalked against him. Then he'd simply dropped out of Soviet life, that was all. But as a precaution he had returned to Russia as a tourist. That way no questions were asked. He'd simply submitted an itinerary and a few dates, pre-booked a hotel or two and the visa was his. Admittedly, the application form had asked an awkward question about former nationality, but he had managed to side-step that one. However, as a tourist there were handicaps. Only certain places in the USSR were open to him (fortunately including Khabarovsk); the State tourist organization to which he was bound was little more than a method of surveillance and those frightful hotels full of little men pretending to be guides.

Lomas said he preferred to explore the town on his own, thank you. The sleek little man in an oversize suit had shrugged and retired hurt. The exchange had taken place in English. Lomas was taking no chances. Though he found it easy to slip back into his mother tongue he forbore to do so in his dealings with *Intourist*. It was, he told himself, simply another precaution.

Lomas left the hotel soon after midday. He thought he could find Lermontov Street without great difficulty. It was pleasant to be out in the town after the confinement of aeroplane and hotel. He turned out of the Square into Karl Marx Street and idled up the pleasant, tree-lined thoroughfare. If you blinkered yourself severely enough it was possible to imagine Khabarovsk to be a city of western Europe. But the comparison kept tumbling into absurdity. The shops were drab, lifeless things, made colourful only by the number of people in them; the roads were sparse of traffic and what there was consisted solely of taxis and commercial vehicles thirty years out of date. But Lomas was seeing with eyes that notched up another comparison. For a city in the great outback Khabarovsk was an eye-opener. Twenty years ago it had not been like this. That way the comparison was equally startling. In those days the fear was a tangible thing. You could see it in the eyes of all who passed by; worn like a badge of Soviet citizenship. He could remember it even in the intimacy of his own family circle; the manner his father used to look at him when he came home from school. Denunciation came with the algebra in those times. But Lomas was not taken in. The evil that had killed his mother still lurked. It wore kid gloves and had become more subtle in its dealings. Even as he strolled beneath the limes he smelt its noxious presence.

Khabarovsk is a city of cubes. Cubic buildings and streets like a chess board. Within an hour Lomas had found Lermontov Street without even an enquiry. It was a short cul-de-sac and no trees graced its uneven pavements. Number 38 was the same as 37 and 39, an apartment of flats that turned living into an industry. Twice he walked slowly past the door.

Having run his quarry to earth, Lomas was at a loss. To wait until Kunetsov emerged and then accost him in the street had been one idea. But maybe Kunetsov was out, maybe he was away for a week or a month. What would he do then? And here the questions began to multiply, as did the permutations. He hadn't really liked the street-accosting idea. It was too public; there were too many distractions. Surely theirs was an intimate affair.

Lomas made up his mind. Squaring his

shoulders he strode up to number 38. At the entrance he was confronted by a battery of bell-pushes each labelled with a name. From the cyrillic lettering he learnt that the Reprostovich household resided on the second floor. He pushed the Reprostovich bell.

The door unlocked itself with a click that invited him to enter. Stone stairs, chipped and worn, bore his footsteps upwards. A smell that might have been stale cabbage soup pervaded the building. From a half-open door giving on to the small landing a girl stood expectantly watching.

Lomas walked up to her, smiling. The brown eyes challenged his own, but were round with inquiry.

For the first time in the Soviet Union he spoke Russian.

'I'm looking for Comrade Reprostovich.' He had nearly said Kunetsov. He must watch it.

The brown eyes continued to hold him.

'He's at his office. He won't be back until six o'clock.' She spoke quietly with a faint lilt of challenge.

Lomas found himself becoming aware of the girl. Her face, even when contorted by the severe countenance, hesitated between plainness and beauty. She was more than a girl, too. Lomas guessed she was pushing thirty. And Jewish. Perhaps that was the reason for the suspicion.

'I'd better come back.'

The girl relaxed slightly. Curiosity was becoming the new emotion.

'Can I help? Perhaps you'd like to leave a message. I'm his daughter.'

'It's kind of you,' replied Lomas, 'but my business is with your father. But I would like – could I talk with you?' He suddenly wanted her to smile.

Instead she looked startled, though the antagonism had evaporated.

Lomas floundered on. 'Actually I'm British. I'm – I'm just visiting Khabarovsk and I think I know your father.'

He realized afterwards that these remarks would hardly inspire the normal Russian to issuing an invitation into his home.

Lomas got his smile. It transformed her. The plainness dropped away but the beauty that remained was not a classical beauty. His eyes skipped over the long waist and legs. She wore flat ballet shoes to reduce her height, though she needn't have bothered. He didn't approve of the way she'd clipped her hair short.

The door was pushed open and she stood aside.

'Can I get you some refreshment?' she asked, leading him into the small living-room.

'Thank you, I've had lunch.' It was a lie, but he didn't want to be in Kunetsov's debt.

The smell of cabbage soup ended with the closing of the door.

Inside was a new world. The flat might have been small, but by Russian standards it was extremely comfortable. The Chinese prints on the wall were good. The furniture was modern and expensive, probably Czech. The sofa on to which he was guided was voluptuous. Obviously Kunetsov was a man to be reckoned with.

'Visitors to Khabarovsk are rare,' she began. Quite obviously what she wanted to say was, 'What the hell do you want?'

From the deep embrace of the sofa Lomas looked up at this girl, this woman, who was having a disturbing effect upon him. All his life women had taken a back seat in his activities. Never had they intruded, had they been allowed to intrude into the affairs of his mind. Of course, he'd admired the mini-skirted legs that twinkled across Waterloo Bridge as the offices opened and, with

Faraday, had ogled the 'crumpet' as it lined up to buy sandwiches at the little bar round the corner from the agency. Once through a desire to conform more than any other form of desire, he'd got himself caught up with a little temp. from accounts. But he'd found she collected men as a hobby and the denouement had been both painful and unpleasant. He'd shied away from women after that.

For a few seconds Lomas made no attempt to explain his presence. He was looking for the first time at her clothes. She wore an all black *après-ski* outfit more like a skin-tight track-suit with a thonged belt. Plain nudity would have been less explicit. He envisaged a desire to prolong the interview.

The girl had seated herself upon a leather pouffe, drawing up her knees and binding them with her arms. Strangely the long silence had produced no embarrassment.

'English visitors who come halfway across the world to see your father are probably rare.'

'But you're Russian, surely? No English-man could speak Russian as well as you do.'

Lomas decided it was not simple flattery. She was intelligent, this one. She'd probably recognized his Ukranian accent.

'I was born in Russia, yes. But I've lived most of my life in England.' He decided the explanation would do for the moment. He didn't want to get too involved in life histories.

'May I ask you what it can be that brings you all the way to see my father? He was in England himself last year. He could have saved you the bother.' The smile injected the beauty back into her face.

'It's a long story,' said Lomas, without any intention of telling it. 'I think we met, he and I, just after the war. He was in the army then, I think?'

It was a clumsy bit of fishing and he knew it. The girl didn't fall for it either. Instead she swung the conversation back to him.

'You've not told me your name.'

'It's Lomas.'

'Is that your first or second name?'

'Just Lomas, and yours?' He could play it that way, too.

'I'm called Inga.'

'Nice name.'

The hostility was back and he couldn't think of anything else to say.

Inga began to uncurl herself. Desperately Lomas probed for words.

'What does your father do?'

'He's manager of a department at the Amur Cable Works.' She looked at him quizzically again. 'Didn't you know that?'

'Oh, I'm not here on business,' answered Lomas hurriedly.

This time the silence *was* embarrassing.

'What do you do?' he asked presently. He really did want to know.

Inga settled down again on the pouffe. 'I'm a jack of all trades. I do a bit of teaching in the Lenin University. In the summer I work part-time with Intourist doing a little interpreting and looking after tourists. I speak some English and some Japanese, but most of my tourists are Japanese and occasionally American, all in transit to or from Japan and none of them interested in Khabarovsk.'

For the first time she laughed. It was an infectious laugh that was as attractive as the smile.

'And you're not married?' Lomas tried to make the question not sound impertinent and succeeded.

Inga looked at the floor and spoke quietly. 'I was engaged once. A railway engineer from Kharkov. We were very much in love and had wonderful plans for the future. It would have meant my leaving Khabarovsk and going to live in the western part of the country. I should have liked that.'

'You don't like Khabarovsk then?'

'The city itself is not so bad. There is the opera, many theatres, good swimming in the summer, but it is so remote. One gets claustrophobia. You just can't understand.'

'I think I can.'

Inga raised her head and smiled her heart-stopping smile.

'It's four o'clock. Father will be here in two hours. You will stop, won't you? We can have some tea.'

Lomas hardly needed the inducement of tea.

It was ten minutes after six when Kunetsov arrived. He let himself in with a key, so the first indication of his arrival was the sound of the inner door closing. As Inga bounded out to meet him Lomas felt the constriction in his stomach. The moment of truth was at hand.

Yet Lomas felt curiously dissatisfied. The set-up was all wrong and he was not in the right frame of mind. And now Inga had rushed out to warn her father of his presence. Kunetsov would have time to compose himself; to bluff his way through a cover story.

The two hours he had spent with Inga had not been productive. Not as far as Kunetsov was concerned at any rate. Twice he had steered the conversation back to the man's past, even to the extent of revealing glimpses of his own. But Inga had dexterously dodged the issue. That alone perhaps was informative. It showed there was something to hide.

He was aware, however, that in other directions he had triumphed. He tried to tell himself it didn't matter, but it did. Inga obviously liked him. The fact inflated his ego. He despised himself for not being great shakes with the opposite sex and the fact had increasingly bothered him. Life was passing him by. There could be no denying either that he felt something for the Russian Jewess who had plied him with green tea and home-made cakes. Even in the short time of their acquaintanceship she had done something to him. A strange, impulsive desire had welled up inside that the legions of bobbysocks, mini-skirts and hot-pants had never released. Yet Lomas remained dissatisfied. The two emotions in his life, the new and the old, failed to mix. Hate was the old. He wanted it to remain strong and vibrant. Instead it was threatening to become diluted with this ridiculous new thing.

Kunetsov came into the room. His face was set into a mould of friendliness, yet the eyes denied it. The fixed smile failed to mask the suspicion. He stretched out a hand to Lomas.

The voice, when it spoke, was throaty. Age had mellowed the tone but not the characteristic. Lomas could hear it reciting the Potma regulations though the words were different. Now it was saying the equivalent of 'What brings you to this neck of the woods?'

Lomas was unsure how to proceed. Inga was still in the room, reluctant to leave. He knew he couldn't even begin to denounce the man while she was there.

'I think you and I have met before.'

Kunetsov gazed at him uncomprehendingly.

'I'm sorry,' he replied, 'ought I to know you?'

Lomas surrendered to circumstances. How could he do otherwise with Inga hovering there?

'I'm looking for my mother,' he lied. 'It's probably rather like hunting for a needle in

46

a haystack after twenty-five years and I'm pretty certain she died shortly after the war, but I suddenly felt I'd like to make sure.'

'What have I to do with it?' The question was brutal but at least had the effect of removing Inga from the scene. She must have sensed both Lomas's discomfort and her father's rising annoyance. The door closed quietly behind her.

Having started the lie Lomas saw that he would have to continue with it.

'I last saw her in 1955. It is the usual story of those times. She was arrested and convicted of something ridiculous. I think they sent her to Potma.'

He watched the man closely as he mentioned the name of the notorious camp, but not by the batting of an eyelid was there the slightest reaction.

'During the years that followed I made exhaustive enquiries, of course, but they revealed nothing. Then I emigrated to Britain and gave things up. Suddenly, a year ago, I saw you and thought I recognized you as someone arrested the same time as Mother. You might have known her in Potma. It seemed a slight hope.'

Kunetsov's face softened. 'It's all so long ago. So many people came into one's life

47

and then disappeared. Even if I had seen her I doubt if I could separate one little fragment of memory from the thousands that have become a blur.' He was giving nothing away.

'*Were* you at Potma?'

Kunetsov shook his head. 'I remained in the army more than twelve years after the war. I was a regular. We were shuffled about all over the Soviet Union and I had a long spell in the German Democratic Republic. May I ask how you connect your mother with me?'

Lomas was forced to extend the lie further. To reveal his knowledge of the facts would only sever the tenuous link.

'It's all very vague,' he explained. 'I saw you, as I said, about a year ago in a London hotel – you may even possibly remember me helping you through the swing doors – and felt convinced that you were not only someone my mother used to know but were also arrested in the same round-up in Darnitsa.'

'Do you mean to say you've come all the way from London to Khabarovsk on the strength of so slim an idea!'

'Well, in a way, yes. You were a lead and I had to start somewhere.'

'How did you find me?'

'The hotel told me your address.'

Kunetsov became expansive. He offered Lomas a cigarette and poured out two glasses of vodka from a decanter on an ornamental table.

'You will stay to dinner, of course.' Even before Lomas could accept the invitation Kunetsov was shouting for Inga to lay an extra place.

'We live quite simply, Inga and I, you understand. My wife died seven years ago, so I depend a lot upon my daughter. I am out all day at my job and often so is she, but I depend on her all the same. It would be a bad day for me if I lost her.'

A kind of dread had come into his voice with the last words. A thought came to Lomas that Kunetsov could be a formidable father.

They both relapsed into silence, during which they downed their vodkas.

'How long are you in Khabarovsk?' Kunetsov was the first to break the silence.

'A week. I suppose I could extend it if it were necessary. Then I go to Kiev.'

A telephone rang somewhere in the flat. A moment later Inga put her head round the door to tell her father he was wanted.

Kunetsov excused himself and left the room. Inga apologized likewise, saying that something was boiling over in the kitchen.

Lomas was alone in the room. He broke away from the sofa's embrace and strolled round the room examining the prints on the wall. On a writing desk near the window a number of small photographs in silver frames caught his eye. One in particular. Right at the back it showed a man in military uniform against an out-of-focus background. But the blurred outline struck a chord. As the implications struck home Lomas found himself staring at KGB Major Igor Kunetsov smirking in front of the administrative bloc, Potma Camp.

For Lomas any final doubts that hovered ghostlike at the back of his mind abruptly vanished.

CHAPTER FOUR

The Soviet security system has many ramifications. The organization has undergone many changes of structure, responsibility and name since its conception and emergence, in 1922, from the Chekist operators of the early twentieth century. It became GPU, OGPU, NKVD, NKGB, and, in 1946, split into MVD and MGB. The latter was renamed KGB in 1954 and made responsible for security and intelligence at home and overseas.

Colonel Anatoli Spassky was actually GUKR, an offshoot of KGB dealing with counter-intelligence. As such he was perhaps not technically empowered to deal with Igor Reprostovich's request. But security matters invariably overlapped the various branches assigned their safe-keeping and, anyway, Spassky was always ready to do Reprostovich a favour. Hadn't they been in Potma together and therefore were both members of what could almost be described as an exclusive club. And membership in the

1950s had its own exclusiveness since with the fall from favour of many of those who carried out the then edicts of the State there were precious few members remaining. So when Reprostovich had asked him if they had anything on this Ukranian-born Lomas character he was pleased to pass the query on to files at head office. They had a week to come up with something, but Moscow always did take its time.

Any foreign visitor to Khabarovsk – like anywhere else in the USSR – was, of course, checked against the current files. These had pronounced the Englishman Lomas as 'clean'. This normally would have been the end of the affair and as long as he kept to within the restrictions of State security he could be classed as a welcome guest with *Intourist*, directly responsible for his movements. Spassky was human enough to ponder briefly upon the reasons for his friend's interest in this particular tourist. But the mere fact that Reprostovich had vouchsafed no information was enough for him. Most of the surviving 1950 membership had items of dirty washing to hide even if not everyone changed their name.

CHAPTER FIVE

During the four days that followed the visit to the Kunetsov flat Lomas learnt much about Inga. With the end of the tourist season she had been able to take time off and had insisted upon accompanying him with almost aggressive intent. They had played all the childish amusements concentrated in the park that rolled down to the Amur. They had strolled arm in arm in the groves of the Khekhuir Hills behind the town. And they had held hands surreptitiously in the dark of three of the city's cinemas. He had never been invited back to the flat, but this he had at first surmised was in deference to the Soviet attitude to foreign visitors. Instead, however, she had flaunted her British friend in the streets of Khabarovsk, cocking a snoot, as it were, at the authorities.

The sun had smiled warmly upon these proceedings and Lomas had been gratified to learn that the autumn was an exceptional one for the Soviet Far East. It was on the fourth such afternoon in a grove of larches on the edge of the *taiga* that Inga unburdened herself.

They lay together upon a carpet of dying bracken. The noises of Khabarovsk had sunk to a soft murmur through which drifted the sounds of the forest. Sunshine turned the trunks of distant silver birches into shafts of steel. Slightly uncertain of the reaction, Lomas drew the girl towards him and, to his surprise, found himself capable of the most passionate kisses. To his further surprise and infinite delight, there was plenty of collaboration.

He looked quizzically down at Inga, his head on one side, as if to say where do we go from here. The haunting fragile beauty of her face was radiant, but clouded by tears in the wide brown eyes. Her breasts heaved in emotion straining at the tight material sheathing the lithe body. His light-headedness turned to concern.

'Why, Inga, what's wrong? You're crying.'

The smile broke through the storm. Self-conscious of the exhibition, she buried her head in Lomas's chest. His arm protectively and more assuredly held her close to him.

'Sorry,' she said after a pause. 'You must think me an awful fool.' She fell back on to the bracken and stared upwards at the vivid blue of the sky. 'The trouble with me is that every time I find happiness it all has to collapse around my ears.'

Lomas remembered the Kharkov engineer. 'What happened last time?' he asked.

'He went the way of any boy-friend I show more than passing interest in.'

Lomas said nothing, trying to puzzle out the conundrum.

'It's my father,' she went on. 'Since Mother died I have become a substitute, at least to all outward appearances. I have to be around to cook his meals and grace his home when guests come. Only for the annual holiday pilgrimage to his sister in Moscow do I get opportunity to escape. You just can't imagine how fiercely possessive he can be. I'm virtually a prisoner of Khabarovsk. How I hate the place.'

'Why don't you break away?'

'With Father and I there's an odd sort of relationship. It's difficult for you to understand. He's spoiling my life, yet I'm incapable of spoiling his. There are other factors, too.'

'What are they?'

'We're Jewish and in the Soviet Union, in spite of what they say, this is not so good. But, more important, there is Father's guilty secret.'

Lomas's heart skipped a beat. He waited, his mind teetering on the brink of a precipice.

'Something happened while he was in the army. I don't know what it was, but I think it preys on his mind. I've heard him talking in his sleep. With a thing like that inside of him how can I leave him?'

Lomas was on the verge of coming out with his dramatic announcement, but managed to restrain himself. It was a question of priorities. His mind in a whirl, he turned to Inga and forced her to look at him.

'What would you say if I asked you to?'

The implication took time to sink in.

'You mean – you mean return with you to England?'

'That's the general idea.'

'But they won't allow it – the authorities, I mean.'

'As a friend, no; as a wife, it's not impossible.'

Inga's face was a study of delighted bewilderment.

'You're not being serious. You can't mean–'

'I'm asking you to be my wife.'

Through the silence that greeted this pronouncement the strident blare of a factory siren penetrated. It seemed to topple Inga from the pedestal of her dreams.

'Oh, darling, what a wonderful thing to say. What can I do?'

'Say yes.'

'What I mean is, how can I even think of going to England with Father still around. You'll be leaving in three days' time. I'll be alone with him again. And all the formalities of application to marry a foreigner. He would never allow it.'

The tears had returned to her eyes and her hand gripped Lomas's with fierce sorrow. She may be Jewish, thought Lomas, but she's also Russian. He was surprised that he was still capable of impersonal observation.

'I could ask him.'

'It would do no good. Your stay in Khabarovsk is nearly up. Even if you got an extension it could only prolong the agony. Father has got the State on his side, too. Our government doesn't approve of foreign marriages.'

Lomas decided it was time for the second pronouncement. This one was calculated.

'What would you say if I told you I knew your father's dark secret?'

Inga stared with frightened eyes.

'What do you mean?'

'It's the reason for my journey to Khabarovsk. Your father murdered my mother.'

During the second silence a slight breeze rustled the foliage, sending down early victims of approaching winter. Both Inga and Lomas felt the cold stab of night.

Next morning Inga had a class at the university so was unable to meet Lomas until midday. They had arranged to lunch together at his hotel. Both grudged the precious hours they would be apart, though each was aware that it would give them breathing space to think.

For Lomas a new challenge had entered his life. Yesterday baring hearts with a good-looking girl alone in the dramatic *taiga* the idea of marriage had seemed a natural culmination of events. Now he was not so sure. Being tied to a woman, living in a country that was not their own, would make him feel so vulnerable. His salary, too, had been nothing to shout about even when he had *had* a job, and here he was living on his small capital. That he was a bit of a rolling stone – and a loner – he was aware, and in the circumstances maybe it was better that way.

On the other hand Inga had pierced his

armour. He was deeply attracted to her; *loved* her, if you like. Having found her, he wanted to have her around, to show her off to his few friends and prove to them he was not the 'queer' he was sure many of them believed him to be.

But it was neither the economic or emotional reasoning that was to sway the balance for Lomas. She was a Soviet citizen, daughter of a respected, even distinguished party member and executive, and doing a useful job herself. True she was a Jew, but she wasn't bellyaching to go to Israel. They weren't going to let her go anywhere for sure. Nor was her father. Lomas saw they had a fight on their hands. This was the real challenge. And he thrived on challenges. He'd been mounting them all his life.

And Kunetsov. What about him? There was a challenge that had turned sour. Kunetsov had become an 'also ran'. But no, this mustn't happen. Lomas balled his fist and slammed it into the palm of the other hand. His mother's murder was *not* to go unavenged. Maybe by taking the girl away he could extract it, excruciatingly. Sort of kill two birds with one stone. A thin smile crossed his face.

For the eleventh time Lomas completed a

circuit of Komsomolskaya Square, built around the standard obelisk to the conquering heroes of the civil war. But it was the last. The next move, metaphorically speaking, for once seemed clear. He thought he could see a short way through the fog of his own indecision.

With brisk steps he made for the hotel.

Inga had spent a sleepless night. Her Japanese class had suffered, too. Yesterday had been a red-letter day in her life and its developments could not be conveniently pushed aside for lesser commitments. A clinical mind had Inga. For the hundredth time she attempted to analyse her emotions. Lomas. She rolled the name round her tongue. He was a nice guy, though she couldn't truthfully say she was head-over-heels in love with him. A bit of a cold fish in a way, but she preferred his sort to those sloppy senior students, ten years her junior, who sometimes came begging for bed. But wasn't she evading an issue? Didn't the prospect of leaving Khabarovsk and the USSR have a heavy bearing on her feelings? Maybe, but if she had to leave her country with anyone it might as well be Lomas. She could admire a man with a strength of purpose like his. Perhaps the love would come later.

And Papa? There was the fly in the ointment. To her he was a bigger hurdle than the State. She was bound to him with an emotional strand that was stronger than she cared to admit. Pity came into it a little, for he was alone in the world and nursed his ghastly secret that was a secret no longer. Maybe there were others. Inga shivered. Yes, fear came into it, too. She had always been a little frightened of the grim-faced man who had taken over from her mother. Even if she could ignore the pity there would be the fear. He would have to know about her proposed marriage and the months of waiting for permission to leave the country would be unbearable. She doubted, too, if he would allow it to get that far. Powerful friends had Papa.

Lomas would know what to do. She was suddenly putting every card she had upon Lomas. But he must not break Papa's heart with the knowledge of his guilt. She couldn't allow that. She would try to transfer some of the love for her father to Lomas, but not at the expense of Papa's happiness. No, Lomas would have to come up with something clever. God, how she depended upon Lomas.

Irrationally she found herself thinking of Pyotr. Her erstwhile fiancé had not been a strong character at all. Before Papa he had fallen at the first fence. But Pyotr could love; how he could love, that one. True, she'd had to teach him; bait him in fact. She remembered the occasion like yesterday. It had happened in his bed-sitter. She'd taunted him to no avail, then lost her temper and picked up a paper-knife. That had done it. Pyotr had caught her arm and twisted it back. The blade had fallen from her hand. She was upon him in an instant, clawing, scratching, kicking, beating. Tears had rolled down her cheeks. Pyotr had lifted her up and thrown her on the bed. There she'd tried to kick him, but he had brushed her legs aside and pinned her to the mattress. She was breathing heavily, tears flowing freely. Her body throbbed with sobs and laughter. He had pressed down on her and pushed his lips against hers. She had shaken her head violently away but he'd caught her hair with one hand and held her face upwards. He gently kissed her and she had submitted. The tears and the sweat had stung her eyes. But it had been magnificent. And that had been only the first time. She

62

wondered how Lomas would score.

Inga managed to dodge the last class of the morning. Political education was compulsory for students and teachers alike, but the instructor had a crush on her. He wouldn't report her absence. As she made for the Dolny Vostok she pondered upon her impending engagement to Lomas. It was ludicrous. Why, she didn't even know his full name!

The dining-room of the Dolny Vostok was less than half full. Nearly all the diners were Russians; foreign guests staying at the hotel being few. It was a long, low room with tables too close together. Glass chandeliers, only a proportion of their electric bulbs working, hung from the ceiling providing another obstruction for waiters to dodge. Small windows, heavily draped, let in a minimum of natural light.

Lomas had met Inga in the vestibule. They kissed awkwardly, aware that *Intourist* staff took note of such incidents. Upon entering the dining-room a waiter had tried to segregate them to a little room at the back reserved for foreigners, but they ignored him. There were important things to talk about and small back rooms, however intimate, could be 'bugged'.

The meal, from any point of view, was not a raving success. Inga had called the waiter a savage for bringing two courses at once to save his footsteps, and the wine, supposed to be Georgian, was some local muck. Over very indifferent coffee the two got their heads together.

Lomas came straight to the point.

'Well, are we or are we not engaged to be married?'

Inga smiled a half-eager, half-sad smile.

'I want to say we are; to shout it from the housetops. But whatever you think of him I have to consider my father.' It was on the tip of her tongue to unload some sob-stuff about him being alone in the world; in need of his daughter's services and all that, but, with Lomas, she knew it wouldn't wash.

'I'm asking you to marry *me* not your father.'

'I know. But I can't marry anyone at the expense of Papa's misery.'

'Doesn't he think at all of his daughter's happiness?'

'I'm not excusing him. I agree he's being selfish. But he's my father and I have a duty to him.'

'You mean he wants you to become an old

maid and continue as his servant.'

'I think if I fell in love with a Khabarovsk man he wouldn't raise any objections.'

'So that you could then be servant for *two* men. But I thought you said it was he who ended your last affair?'

'Yes, I suppose it was, though Pyotr didn't really try very hard. Anyway, he came from Kharkov and that, like London, is the other side of the world.'

Lomas found that brutality was getting him nowhere. He would have to try a little reasoning.

'I think the next thing is for me to speak to your father.'

A hint of pain came into Inga's eyes.

'What do you want to say to him?'

'The things a prospective bridegroom usually asks of a prospective bride's father. It's being a bit old-fashioned I suppose, but in this instance I'm prepared to try it.'

'You won't bring up that matter of your mother?' she asked, full of anxiety.

'Not unless he turns me down.'

'Lomas, no. On no account must you mention it.'

Lomas began to show anger.

'You can't have your cake and eat it. He did kill my mother, you know. I'm prepared to forget it as far as he's concerned on condition he kicks up no fuss about you marrying me. I'm not asking much, you must admit.'

Inga buried her face in her hands. For a moment Lomas thought she was crying, but it was simple frustration. He touched her arm.

'Right, then, no mention but also no ifs and buts. You'll just proceed with the formalities of getting permission to marry me and to hell with him.'

'Yes, I think I could do that, but how do I know he won't resist it behind my back even if not openly? I told you he's got many friends and some of them are in the police. They have a big say in things of this kind.'

'I *bet* they do.'

The anger had turned to bitterness as Lomas's mind picked itself up before the brick wall of the problem. He'd gone over it all a score of times even without Inga to supply the verbal objections. He knew, too, that whether or not he revealed his secret to Kunetsov made little difference. They were in a country where you couldn't just walk out with a girl citizen you wished to marry. Even if she got as far as lodging an application in the right quarters, the State, with the connivance of her father, would ensure it didn't stick. Nor would he, Lomas, be allowed back into the country to stir matters up. The thing would simply die in a welter of red tape.

Arm in arm they strolled along the concrete ramparts that restrained the town from falling into the river. Darkness came early in September and already there was an icy nip in the air. Half-hearted illumination from street lamps sparked off the frozen dew on the grass so that it was like walking through a field of fireflies. There was no moon but the lights of Khabarovsk threw yellow fingers on to the water, fingers that groped for the opposite bank lost in darkness and distance.

Few people were about except furtive couples like themselves. Inga shivered and Lomas drew her closer to him. They walked in silence, having exhausted all approaches to the one subject that occupied their minds. As they turned into the streets Inga spoke in a voice heavy with defeat.

'I nearly forgot. As it's your last day, Papa has invited you to dinner tomorrow. You can have a swim with him in the Amur before-hand if you like. He's a great one for swimming, is Papa, and this fine spell has prolonged it for him. He has a favourite spot a kilometre out of town. He'll pick you up in the car.'

The celebration dinner, thought Lomas. The victor showing his magnanimity to the vanquished. Not only had Kunetsov killed his mother but was also throttling his first real love affair.

'Are you coming – swimming I mean?'

'No, it's too cold for me. Anyway, I've the meal to cook.'

'Of course, you're the skivvy, aren't you?'

All he could find was bitterness.

It was not until after he had kissed Inga goodnight and was walking back through the silent streets towards his hotel that the significance of Kunetsov's invitation struck home. There, served up on a plate, was the noose for Kunetsov's neck. It was almost as if Inga was testing him; daring him to take the only remaining course open to them.

In his excitement Lomas broke into a trot. He wondered if he'd have the guts to take it; to ensure that only two of them sat down to dinner that very next evening of their lives.

CHAPTER SIX

The spot that Kunetsov had selected for his summer bathing was well chosen from all points of view. A small beach of grey sand bordered a clearing in the great carpet of trees that here marched straight to the water's edge. A rough track led them to it from the road that wound out of the suburbs of Khabarovsk.

Kunetsov had collected Lomas from the hotel in a small new Fiat. That he had a car at all, let alone a foreign make, offered visible proof of Kunetsov's status in the community. The smirk on his face showed he wanted Lomas to know it.

'I've bought a pair of trunks for you,' he had said.

'Many thanks,' replied Lomas, climbing into the front seat. 'I'm a bit of a swimmer myself, but hardly expected a dip in Siberia.'

Actually Lomas was a very good swimmer. The one time he deigned to take part in a team event back home was with a Southwark swimming club to which he belonged.

They spoke little as the concrete of the city centre gave way to sad little wooden *Izba* houses made gay with flags of washing that hung from upstairs windows. It was late afternoon and the warmth of the sun was beginning to wane. The tarmac of the road became patchy and Kunetsov concentrated upon dodging the pot-holes. Once he made an excuse for the bad surface.

They turned into the track, which was not much worse than the road.

'This is a good spot for a swim,' pronounced Kunetsov, trying to whip up friendly relations. 'Not many people come here even in mid-summer. They prefer the large beaches nearer the town.'

Lomas mumbled something. He was not in a sociable mood. He was praying that Kunetsov's little hide-out was secluded enough for his purpose. That it was suitable for murder. Murder. The word sounded novelish, unreal. Premeditated murder. Lomas couldn't take in the fact that he was actually planning to kill another human in cold blood. It was no good trying to plan *how* he would do it. He didn't even know if he *could* do it. He looked sideways at Kunetsov waffling on about his prowess in water.

There wouldn't be a great deal of resistance there. The hulking frame that bullied its way around Potma had gone to seed.

A pot-belly showed through the thick suiting and the nicotine-stained fingers labelled a heavy smoker. No, it wasn't so much the physical act that worried him.

Close to the little beach Kunetsov parked the car. While they undressed at the base of a tree, Lomas, with great effort, waxed enthusiastic about the place. He must put Kunetsov at ease. It would never do to have the man suspicious or on his guard. The sudden volubility had an effect upon Kunetsov. He became conspiratorial.

'You know, Lomas, my daughter likes you,' he said, apropos of nothing. He spoke brightly as if it was a thought that had just entered his head.

'I'm glad of that. She's a nice girl.'

'Inga's a good girl, yes. Sometimes I feel I'm holding her back, but I don't think so. She's not met the right man yet and while she's free I do depend on her so.'

'What would you say if she fell for a foreigner?' Lomas was surprised at his own directness.

So apparently was Kunetsov. While removing his socks he subjected Lomas to a long scrutiny. The eyes were challenging behind the bushy brows.

'I would never let her go.'

He spoke quietly but firmly. There was a threat in the voice that was not lost upon Lomas. They were words that spelt out a death sentence.

In his black trunks Kunetsov made a poor figure of a man. His limbs were big but flabby, the pink flesh bulging over balloons of fat. That he had been strong once showed in the wasted muscles and the protruding sinews of the legs that saw little exercise. Eager to set the example and show his proprietorship of this reach of the river, he strode recklessly into the water. Lomas followed with less vigour. The water was cool but not icy. It was shallow for some distance and, wading after Kunetsov, he was able to pick up a stone about the size of a large orange. Now that the task was inevitable he felt relaxed, his head clear and calm. The hand carrying the stone dangled in the water.

Deep water came abruptly. Kunetsov lunged forward into a showy crawl. For Lomas the strategy whereby he would entice Kunetsov close to him lay with the small piece of rock he held. Unable to exhibit his own style, he floundered after him in a clumsy side-stroke as if he was but an enthusiastic amateur.

Some fifty yards out Kunetsov began to meet the pull of the current. He turned and trod water, watching Lomas's feeble efforts. He was disappointed that he had so amateurish a companion for what was likely to be his last swim of the season. Still, it was good of him to come. He swam slowly back towards Lomas in an exaggerated breast stroke, submerging his head at each sweep of his arms.

They met and both trod water.

'Like it?' asked Kunetsov, pushing back a thin lock of hair spreadeagled across his forehead.

'Fine,' replied Lomas, grinning. 'I'm not exactly a contestant for the Olympics, but I like it all the same.' His grip tightened on the stone.

'Is that Chinese territory over there?' he indicated with his head towards the line of hills fading into the dusk across the water.

Kunetsov turned to look.

Lomas struck.

The rock caught the older man square on the back of the head. It was not a death blow but enough to render Kunetsov unconscious. The head gradually sank from view.

Lomas watched it go, then, having second thoughts, grabbed an arm. He'd better make sure the chap was dead before he released the body. After all, it had been an awkward blow and he could recover. And that would be very awkward indeed. So, treading water, Lomas held on long after the period had elapsed when death was in doubt.

It came to him that he had never witnessed the drowning of a man. Death by this method was supposed to be the most pleasant of deaths. Not that Kunetsov had known anything about it, which, in a way, was a pity. With some revulsion Lomas pulled the corpse to him and allowed the head to break the surface. The black hair was plastered even flatter than usual across the skull. The mouth was open as if in surprise. But the eyes. The eyes were open too, staring at Lomas with a hatred that was alive. They bored into him so that he retreated from it, pushing the thing back beneath the murky waters.

He wished he hadn't looked. The sight had unnerved him, filling him with doubts. It brought home the significance of what he had done. He tried to fill his mind with

74

excuses. He piled them in, desperately trying to hide the death mask that had reproduced itself in his memory. After all, wasn't Kunetsov a criminal? He had murdered his mother. A faint picture of Potma appeared blurred and out of focus, to fall before the image of an Inga with eyes that were Kunetsov's. Damn. No. Potma, Potma, Potma. But Potma wouldn't come. That hatred was as dead as Inga's father. In that instant Lomas knew that he had killed for no other purpose than for the love of a woman.

He shook his head, trying to think rationally. How long was it before bodies came to the surface? He wished he'd studied the subject. Better to push the corpse out into the main current. With luck it would by-pass Khabarovsk and beach hundreds of miles away. The odds were it would never be found. This was a sparsely populated region, remote and untamed. Kunetsov's skeleton would slowly disintegrate into dust like those of the giant mammoths that once hunted these lonely forests.

Swimming slowly, he propelled the body before him. Waterlogged, it threatened to drag Lomas down, turning and twisting as if fighting for life. Feeling the tug of the current, he let it go, half expecting the head to bob to the surface. But, around him, the water remained unbroken.

Abruptly Lomas realized how cold he was. Turning, he made for the shore using a steady crawl. He swam obliquely towards the little beach, surprised at the undertow. His mind was clear again. He would quickly dress and slip back into town, leaving Kunetsov's clothes where they were. In that deserted spot they would not be found until the man's absence had been noticed. The police would then put two and two together and make four. Death by drowning would look better on the records than an unsolved disappearance. He tried to think who might have noticed them together. Possibly someone at the hotel, though there was no indication of their going swimming. He would have a story ready in case.

Inga. How would she react to the news of her father's death? He would go straight to the flat and tell her, of course. Cramp, that was the cause. Cramp could strike anyone and Papa was not so young as he was. The water was cold, too. He would be deeply upset and stricken with grief to match her own. If she wanted it so, they could report the matter to the police. He would not stop her. But he would point out that it would assuredly complicate their plans. He thought the carrot of the West would be a very potent vegetable in her case.

His feet struck shingle. Shivering, Lomas emerged alone from the water.

The return to the city had posed a problem. The car would have to remain where it was, forming part of the props of Kunetsov's demise. So Lomas had had to walk, making a considerable detour to avoid being seen in the vicinity of the Kunetsov beach. It had taken longer than anticipated and he was worried that Inga might have started making enquiries.

In the event Lomas was just in time. With no key, he had to ring the flat bell. Inga, wearing an apron over her housecoat, answered it, the relief at seeing him at first blinding her to the shock implanted upon Lomas's face.

'Where have you been? The meal's ruined. Papa's putting the car away, I suppose. Couldn't he have left it until afterwards?'

Lomas made no reply. Inga glanced at him and went white.

'Lomas! What's happened?'

'Inga darling, it's your father. He – he's got

drowned. He swam out too far and got cramp. I went after him, but he was gone before I could reach him. I dived and dived but couldn't find him. What else could I do?' Lomas piled on the agony.

Inga sat down on a chair and stared at nothing.

'Oh, God,' was all she could say. She looked stunned and frightened. No tears had come to her eyes. After the shock would come the remorse, thought Lomas. Then the tears. Or at least they should do. If she was as good at acting as he was. He was surprised how cynical he was becoming. Maybe she wasn't acting. Maybe she hadn't really expected this solution to their problems. All he did know was that they would both have to go through the motions of grief. The truth must remain a secret they could never share. For him to reveal his true actions; for her to tell of her connivance – however passive – would kill stone dead any love existing between them.

Lomas put an arm around the slender waist and covered a hand with his own. It brought the tears but also a response to his silent confirmation of adoration. Her hand gripped his own and she looked up into his face.

'What are we going to do?' she whispered.

Lomas was careful not to rush into practicalities. It would be better, he thought, if suggestions for the next move came from her. He put on a bewildered, hopeless expression.

'I suppose we must tell the police. It'll mean all sorts of complications and unpleasantness, but it can't be helped.'

'Yes, of course. They'll alert the boat patrol and make a search. Perhaps – perhaps he managed to get ashore further down the bank.' The hope in her voice dried the tears and she started up, intent about going to the telephone in her father's study.

Lomas cursed to himself. He hadn't meant her to react quite so fast.

'I'm quite sure he never surfaced,' he said quietly. 'On a sheet of water like that you can see for miles. Going to the police will mean that we can never be together again. But if it has to be–'

'Wait, no not that. With Papa gone I can't lose you too. Yet to do nothing is– Oh, Lomas, I'm so confused and frightened.'

The tears came unchecked now. Inga turned away, aware even through her grief that the make-up on her face was suffering. She ran into her bedroom and flung herself on the bed.

Lomas heard her sobbing. He resisted the impulse to follow. Best let her get this bit over alone, he decided. He went to the living-room and sat down on the pouffe. Things were going well. She hadn't allowed her father's death to stampede her into anything foolish. To have reported the thing to the police would have been most unwise. His – Lomas's – interest in Inga would not have gone unnoticed. Kunetsov might have aired his opinions of potential sons-in-law to someone and a dead father-in-law could set them thinking. Particularly when his daughter started submitting applications to marry the said son-in-law. Even as things were at present, an absent father-in-law would be bad enough. He began to contemplate the next move. In the morning he would leave for Irkutsk. His westbound aircraft landed there anyway so he'd shoved a 48-hour stop-over on to his itinerary. He wished he hadn't now, but it was too late to ask *Intourist* to alter schedules. Better to have gone straight to Kiev. He'd got a week there. He wondered how many of his relations and friends were still around in that city. In the bad old days it had been unwise to maintain contact, so he'd got out of the habit. Maybe Inga could join him in

Kiev. Perhaps they could get permission to go together to Moscow there to put in motion the formalities of her marriage to a foreign national. Lomas grimaced to himself. He supposed he *was* a foreign national. Marriage. He grimaced again. The institution failed to fill him with the joys of spring. The idea of Inga being around was fine; it would be fun for a bit, but to have her on his neck 'until death doth you part' filled him with a certain amount of dismay. He shook off the momentary depression. All that was a long way ahead and still in the realms of conjecture. First catch your hare.

The door opened and Inga entered. Her eyes were dry and she had repaired the ravages to her face. A slight smile played about the corners of her mouth.

'I'm all right now,' she said simply. 'I've done with weeping. We must think now of the future, not the past.'

Lomas was lost in wonderment at the transformation. She really looked something, standing there challenging her tragedy and the world. He extended both his arms and she came to him.

'Tomorrow you say you go to Irkutsk. Right, I will go there too. Perhaps not on the same aircraft, but there will be others. It will not be difficult. Papa has – had – influence in this town.' She moved into his arms aggressively, allowing one breast to brush his face as she leaned over Lomas to kiss the top of his head.

Still perched on the pouffe, he dragged the girl down and rolled with her on to the carpeted floor. He heard her hard breathing and knew that she wanted him to hurt her as an antidote to the mental pain she had experienced. He knew, too, that he was on trial. Perhaps she was thinking of Pyotr.

Lomas was aware that he was not good at this sort of thing. Lack of experience, he supposed. He preferred, too, the comfort and seclusion of a bed. The sedate furniture and the classy prints on the wall offered a despising audience. He caught sight of the photograph of Major Kunetsov staring disapprovingly from its frame. Something hit Lomas from within and the surge of passion became a kind of revenge.

They had nothing to say to each other. Deftly, yet without appearing to be doing so intentionally, Inga allowed the long housecoat she had been wearing to fall away, revealing her lean body with feline arrogance. The gentle glow from the table lamp illuminated for a moment the white skin before Lomas was upon her. Just for a moment, before her ecstatic whimper, he wondered stupidly why she wore no underclothes.

It was quite dark outside when they dined *tête à tête* in the kitchen. The meal was not overcooked in spite of the alleged delay. There was just the right amount for the two of them.

They discussed ways and means of meeting up in Irkutsk. Inga knew the town and the fact that there were only two *Intourist* hotels to which Lomas could be assigned to stay.

'I'll meet you at the "Siberia". It'll probably be that one,' she had vouchsafed.

Lomas was more cautious. 'Why not give Irkutsk a miss and come straight to Kiev. I have to go to Irkutsk, but only for a couple of days.' It was occurring to him that it might be more prudent of Inga not to follow him around.

He was unprepared for the whiplash of her retort.

'Listen, Lomas. From now onwards I intend hardly leaving your side. I'm coming back with you to England however we have to play it. *I've got you for better or for worse.*'

As she spoke her knee pressed his thigh

beneath the table. For the life of him Lomas was unable to make out whether her words were an endearment wrapped in a threat or the other way around.

CHAPTER SEVEN

With studied deliberation Colonel Spassky read through the report that had come in from Moscow. He came to the end and read it again. A methodical man was Anatoli Spassky. Some called him a plodder, which wasn't a bad description. But though slow on the uptake he may sometimes have been, his method and his attention to detail paid dividends both for the State and for himself. He had fought and won a decoration at Stalingrad before a wound knocked him out of the war. Being a professional soldier, he had accepted an administrative job in the camps as the lesser of many evils that civilian life could offer. The fact that it was a semi-military organization made his task as regional inspector at least bearable. He did not approve of the camps or the reasons for them, but these opinions he kept to himself. He had met Igor at Potma not long before the reduction of the penal settlements and it was, of course, Igor who had got him his present police job. Igor was a sly one. He had seen the change of policy coming and fixed himself a plum appointment in industry. True, it had been in territory looked upon as the 'great outback', but it was a gamble that had paid off. Khabarovsk had developed into quite a reasonable sort of place considering. And it was he who had used influence to get him – Spassky – into the Security ranks of the KGB. If you were prepared to accept the early rigours of the 'great outback' good jobs were not hard to get, but for State Intelligence one still needed a sponsor. All things considered, he owed Igor much.

For his years Anatoli Spassky was a good-looking man. His rugged face had a leathery quality that intimated a clean, open-air life. He had retained his neat military moustache and clipped form of speech. He never walked but strode even with the impediment of a gammy leg that produced a slight limp. Tall and lithe, even in middle-age, he had all the attributes of a military man except for a pair of the sleepiest blue eyes imaginable. Many a man – NCO or junior officer – had misjudged those eyes, to be brought up sharp with swift reprimand. Like his slow reactions, the tolerant eyes were deceptive. Spassky had never married anything except his job, and into this he poured his whole being. If he had a family in his native Kursk nobody could recollect him visiting it.

He came to the end of the second reading. So they had something on this Englishman Lomas or whatever he called himself. Once it seemed he had been Ilyich Palatnik of Kiev, and he'd done 'time' for collaboration with the enemy during the Great Patriotic War. Then he'd gone to Finland and from there had emigrated west. Spassky's thin lips curled at the word 'collaboration', but, upon reflection, he revised his opinion. 'Collaboration' – especially in the Ukraine – was a useful label in those days to pin on anybody someone wanted putting away for a bit. Anyway, he'd served his punishment. The fact that he had gone West was his only other indiscretion. In this particular circumstance the action was hardly worth investigating. Personally he'd have let the thing go. But if Igor wanted something on this Lomas fellow, well, there it was. He put through a call to the Amur Cable Works.

The voice at the other end said that Comrade Reprostovich had not been at the office all day. It was all very odd, for he had an engagement with an important client and it was not like him at all to be away without telling his secretary. Yes, of course they'd rung his home. They'd even sent someone round.

Spassky rang his friend's private number. He listened a considerable time to the ringing tone before replacing the receiver. Remembering the daughter, he tried the university. He was passed through several departments and finally got a woman who, with some indignation, announced the fact that the girl had not been in all day. 'Missed two Japanese classes just like that without even bothering to phone if you please,' the voice added before he cut it off.

He tried a new tack. Dialling a third number, he learnt from *Intourist* that the Englishman Lomas had left that morning on the scheduled flight to Irkutsk. 'Was he alone?' he had asked. The voice assured him that he was.

A less methodical man would have left it there. After all, if Igor and his daughter wanted to play truant and take the day off, who was he interfere? But Spassky knew his man. The absence from work was out of character. He didn't like the smell of things.

He rang the airport and asked for Departures.

'Anyone by the name of Reprostovich left

Khabarovsk today?' he enquired.

There was some delay as a list was consulted.

'Yes, for Irkutsk.'

'What plane did he catch?'

'It was a woman. She left on the special afternoon service. Only an hour ago in fact.'

Spassky replaced the receiver. His blue eyes grew small as if sleep had come unbidden from a drug. He sat lost in thought a full sixty seconds, then dialled a final number.

Maybe it was coincidence that Igor's daughter should have gone to Irkutsk too. Even if not, it was hardly any business of his. Anyway it was not a security case, but he'd have a word with the criminal boys all the same. They could keep an eye on each of them, report on their movements and so on. Yes, the criminal boys at Irkutsk would know what to do.

CHAPTER EIGHT

Trees, trees in all directions. A great suffusion of trees that spread to every horizon. Here and there tiny clearings marking a hamlet ensnared in the interminable morass held the eye, each flaunting a hopeless existence at the end of a ribbon of jungle track that fluttered into oblivion.

In the giant TU winging westwards across the time-zones of eastern Siberia the passengers watched in passive silence. Most had seen it all before, but the panorama of loneliness below drew all eyes with sombre fascination. And just when the scene had reached a climax and its captive audience was quietly gauging how much more it could stand, a vivid scar of water slashed the throttling green. Like steam escaping from a safety valve, the whisper spread through the crowded cabin, 'Ah, look, Baikal!' and the spell was broken. Chatting excitedly as if released from some fate unknown, the captive audience of flight SU1841 became individuals once again.

Lomas saw the great lake expand and shrink with distance, its arms of water probing the sullen landscape swathed in twisting scarves of mist. At the end of one of them, astride the majestic Angara river the city of Irkutsk acted as a magnet, drawing all downwards to the myriad silver birches. In a scream of reverse-thrust the aircraft careered along on airport tarmac that had once been oblivion.

A spotty-faced girl of Japanese ancestry met Lomas in the reception lounge. There was no giving *Intourist* the slip. Of that he was sure. He looked around him. Everywhere there were Buryats, Uzbeks and Mongols, all standardized citizens of the USSR. He was more Russian than all of them, yet here was this slit-eyed wench singling him out as a 'foreigner'. A wave of resentment passed through him; resentment tinged, ironically, with a little relief. Lomas was not so Russian as all that. He was assigned to a dilapidated taxi, left to heave his bag into the boot and, the girl with him on the back seat, rattled into the city centre.

Inga was right. The hotel was the 'Siberia'. It was a concrete structure of purely functional appearance, the plaster on the walls cracked and flaking from extremes of temperature. He was ushered to the head of the queue at the reception desk where the usual massive formalities of booking into a Soviet hotel were set in motion. In spite of the distraction caused by the issue of various meal coupons, Lomas caught the brief nod that passed between a man sitting behind a desk and someone close at hand half hidden by the queue. So slight had been the exchange it held no significance.

In his small room on the first floor Lomas spreadeagled himself on the bed and gazed up at the off-white ceiling. The fact he was alone again in a strange city recharged his desire for Inga. There was no denying the fascination she held for him. He tried to analyse his feelings, placing them in little compartments of his mind. Right, he was attracted to the girl: he liked her company and she made a good ride. But all this crap about love and marriage was way over his head. Okay, she had triggered a fresh awareness for women; for women in general. Again the threat of being lumbered with Inga for a wife hovered close. It eclipsed the other worry and the fact that he had recently committed a capital crime bothered him hardly at all. All he had to do as far as that was concerned was to serve the remainder of his stay in the Soviet Union as a good tourist and return home. The only possible danger could materialize from Inga following him about. And what was all that guff about 'coming back to England *however we have to play it?*' When she found him in Irkutsk she would have to clarify this point. He didn't much like the sound of it. Lomas stirred restlessly.

Late in the afternoon he emerged from the hotel for a stroll. Irkutsk was hardly a mecca of inspiration but it did hold a certain Tolstoydian charm that was lacking in Khabarovsk. Lomas wandered down the busy centre made comfortable with 19th century public buildings set amongst tree-lined wide-pavemented street of residential *Izba* houses.

Close to a crossroads he became aware of a man staring at him. People frequently stared; foreigners were not so common in Irkutsk, particularly those with smart leather shoes. But usually they went on staring brazenly and made no attempt to conceal the fact like the man by the tram-stop. Lomas briefly noted the thick suiting and open-necked check shirt. Hadn't he seen the fellow before? He racked his brains for a moment to no avail, then, on the spur of the moment, caught one of the rickety old red trams that afflicted the city streets.

It was a wasted effort. The man made not the slightest attempt to follow, though there was no lack of opportunity. Lomas grimaced to himself, irritated at the sudden attack of nerves that had pushed him into an uncomfortable vehicle when he would have preferred to walk. He alighted at the next stop without paying.

The red ball of a setting sun turned the green copper domes of Irkutsk cathedral into outsize Christmas-tree decorations set against a snowfield of solid white stone. Beneath a tangle of tram cables a police traffic check was in progress, with vehicles filtering through temporary red and white striped barriers. The blue-uniformed patrolmen took not the slightest notice of Lomas crossing the road to walk unnecessarily through the block. As he leisurely made his way back along a High Street made colourless in contrast with a fairy-tale cathedral, Lomas spat contemptuously. To flaunt the guardians of the greatest police-state on earth acted as a heady antidote to a moment of blind panic that had assailed him earlier.

An unappetizing evening meal in a small room set aside for foreigners at the hotel left him at a loose end. What was there to do at night in a city like Irkutsk? He was gloomily contemplating the prospect of going to bed at half-past eight when Inga burst back into his life. She was arguing vigorously with the reception staff and Lomas felt the weight of loneliness lift from his shoulders. If he had to go to bed at half-past eight, at least there would be no need to do so alone.

Lomas was surprised at his own enthusiasm for the girl's return. By her side in an instant, he hugged her with wild abandon, ignoring the unsympathetic audience.

'I didn't think you'd be here till tomorrow,' he exclaimed. 'I was on the verge of committing suicide in this ball-of-fire town.'

Inga smiled her devastating smile but remained calm. 'I was lucky,' she said. 'Normally there's only one flight a day to Irkutsk, but we've a trade fair on in Khabarovsk and they're running two.'

An impatient clerk booked her into a room two floors above Lomas. He was relieved to note that the Hotel Siberia was not – anyway at this time of the year – exclusively *Intourist*.

'The cuisine here hardly rates a star, but its probably better than anywhere else. I've just had a meal, but I'll sit with you while you have yours if you like.'

Inga handed her bag to Lomas. 'We needn't bother,' she said. 'I managed something at the airport.'

Together they went upstairs. The large woman attendant whose domain covered the first floor had vacated her desk, but her colleague on the third floor eyed Lomas with suspicion as she handed Inga the key of her room. Lomas felt obliged to explain he was simply carrying her bag.

Inga's room was a replica of his own. A box of a place holding the bare essentials. A smaller box contained a shower, wash basin and toilet. Inga made use of the wash basin, opened her case and strewed some of her belongings about the bed and dressing-table. She turned to Lomas.

'Let's go down to your room. The old cow out there will be watching us like a hawk until we put her out of her misery.'

Leaving the door unlocked, they moved down the stairs. Lomas found his key in a cubicle above the empty desk at the head of the stairway. He sat down on the bed and watched with mild amazement as Inga, without the slightest hesitation or hint of ladylike coyness, proceeded to divest herself of her clothes. Only as she stepped out of her panties did she murmur, 'You did say,

Lomas dear, there was nothing else to do in this town, didn't you?'

She stood before him naked, a tiny smile that might have been challenge or derision on her face. Lomas stared at her without expression, his eyes resting on the salient points of her body as if he was examining a machine. He liked what he saw, but something made him uneasy. He wasn't used to this high-powered stuff. Old-fashioned methods still guided his movements where sex was concerned. As he removed his tie Lomas experienced the notion that he was about to be raped.

Said Inga, 'You'll have to accept me in the raw. I've left my night things upstairs.' She climbed into bed.

Still uncertain of himself, Lomas climbed in beside her. He felt her eagerness as her hands searched his body. He wouldn't have minded so much perhaps if she'd said please.

The alarm clock that woke them turned out to be the telephone. Its strident demand battered at their sleep, leaving a mounting awareness that was as unwelcome as it was uncouth. That it was broad daylight was Lomas's second discovery, and he looked towards Inga for enlightenment.

'It's your room, you'd better answer it,' she said brusquely. 'It's probably only your *Intourist* guide anyway.'

Lomas slid off the bed conscious of his own nakedness and bending low said 'Hello' into the mouthpiece.

The voice, a million miles away, spoke with a heavy accent. 'Mister Lomas, yes, please to come to the reception at once.'

Irritation boiled in Lomas. 'We, I mean I was asleep. What do you mean by waking me up just for a tour of–'

'Mister Lomas, *please*. It is the police. They want to talk with you. You must come now.' The voice exploded in his ear.

'All right,' he replied, slamming down the receiver. 'It's the police,' he hissed at Inga. 'They're waiting for me below.'

Inga was out of bed in a flash. As she struggled into her clothes Lomas was too occupied with his own hasty dressing to see the crazed light in her eyes.

'I didn't think it would come as quickly as this.' She was talking to herself. 'I'd hoped we could be at least in Kiev before they were on to us. Damn and blast. Now we're on our own, Lomas, like it or not. We'll have to leave our things behind. From now on we're travelling light. My God, Lomas, you'd better have some good friends in Kiev. They're the only ones we're likely to have in the whole cursed Soviet Union.'

Hardly comprehending her words, Lomas stuffed a few necessities into his pockets. Blind panic gripped him again, erasing any assumption that the visitation was simply a routine enquiry. Gone was the Lomas of yesterday who cocked snoops at police traffic checks. What was left showed a frightened man fast becoming aware of the enormity and futility of what he had done. He was bothering now.

If Inga had noticed the transformation she gave no sign. Taking her cue, she had slid into command of the situation and led Lomas swiftly down the back stairs. Already her mind had gauged the magnitude of the opposition and was assessing the chances of evasion. Maybe she had fallen down on one calculation, but otherwise the general strategy was going according to plan.

CHAPTER NINE

Colonel Anatoli Spassky was as surprised as anyone. Irkutsk criminal branch had come on with their version of the flight of this Lomas chap and the Reprostovich girl. Spassky had listened to the indignant tones of the officer over the wire and disapproved of the methods Irkutsk chose to use. He couldn't for the life of him see why they should want to show their cards. Keep them under observation, he had said; not hold a committee meeting with the couple. But at least he now had confirmation that the birds were together even if they had flown.

To all intents and purposes the thing was way outside his domain. But it intrigued him. Igor had wanted something on this Lomas and he – Spassky – had obliged with an unpursued illegal emigration charge. Now Lomas was notching up quite a list of offences – ignoring the orders of a police officer, evasion of *Intourist* supervision, and, possibly, criminally influencing a Soviet citizen. Igor no doubt would be pleased, but for the fact that his daughter had become involved – and even she had absconded from a hotel without paying the bill.

Anatoli Spassky sat lost in thought, doodling on his note-pad. For the second day running he had rung Igor's office and home as well as many of his friend's acquaintances with no positive result. Now all he could do was to await further reports from Irkutsk to shed light on the mystery.

In the event a large chunk of the puzzle fell into place right on his own doorstep.

Captain Kedrov, his personal adjutant, had burst in on top of a perfunctory knock late that afternoon. That something was amiss showed plainly on the man's face, scotching the bark of reprimand that rose unbidden to Spassky's throat.

'What is it, Kedrov?'

'We have found a body, Comrade Colonel. I think you ought to see it.'

Spassky led his adjutant down the stone stairs to the neon-lit morgue in the cellars of the building. A man in a white smock saluted and indicated a concrete slab in the middle of the room. He drew back the sheet to reveal the corpse.

Igor Reprostovich looked peaceful in death. The small laceration on the back of his head was not noticeable until Kedrov had pointed it out. Spassky's face became more inscrutable than ever as he hid a gust of emotion. Only his eyes came suddenly alive.

The doctor's voice provided a dirge. 'Cause of death is drowning, but this occurred after unconsciousness. He must have been in the water about forty hours, which puts the time of death at about four o'clock the day before yesterday.'

Kedrov, in the same flat voice, intoned the police findings. 'A fishing boat found the body near the junction of the rivers. Though, as you see, he was drowned whilst bathing, we can find no reason for the head wound. Had he dived from a boat and struck his head on the river bed it would have been his forehead or at least the top of his head that would have suffered. Incidentally we discovered his car and clothes on the small beach he uses the other side of town. We find signs – unproven – that he went swimming with a companion while the Dolny Vostok Hotel confirms that, late that afternoon, Comrade Reprostovich collected in his car one of their clients, an English tourist called Lomas.'

Spassky turned away from the corpse and

the sheet was replaced. He noticed that Kedrov was respectfully putting two and two together and leaving him to spell out murder. The crime – and surely there were now enough factors to label it thus – had abruptly become not only a personal matter but a security case. Igor had been KGB, and, in that classification, once KGB always KGB.

With a sense of urgency Spassky limped his way up the stone stairs.

CHAPTER TEN

Irkutsk railway station is situated in the suburb of Glazkovskoe on the opposite bank of the Angara river. The river is spanned by a single road bridge. It would be on this bridge, surmised Inga, where they would have the blocks out in the event of even a limited police alert. Not that either of them had reached this stage of notoriety. She hoped they'd never rate it in fact, but her country's police had a disconcerting habit of jumping first and asking the questions afterwards.

As they strode through the back streets behind the hotel, Inga attempted to visualize to herself the action that might be taken against them. Even Lomas recovered his wits enough to contribute some observations. The officer at the hotel would almost certainly give Lomas half an hour before ascending to the room. After all, Lomas was a tourist, which meant that certain niceties had to be maintained. He would then report the matter to headquarters, who would start making enquiries of *Intourist*. And *Intourist* would tell them that a reservation on *Aeroflot* had been booked for tomorrow to Kiev. This might stall them.

The bridge came into sight across a multiple road junction. It was alive with scurrying pedestrians on both pavements and a considerable amount of traffic occupied the road. Not a policeman was to be seen.

Another danger point was the station itself. The odds were heavily against it being overlooked in the lowest possible state of surveillance. But again time was not on the side of the law. Given the chance of a convenient train within, say, half an hour, reckoned Inga, she'd have the Irkutsk police running round in small circles.

They stood looking at the black departures board.

'We're in luck, Inga, look, there's the westbound express departing at 9.30 in just twenty minutes.'

Inga gave Lomas a pitying look.

'It's obvious you've not been a Soviet citizen for many years,' she said scathingly. 'Don't you know that reservations are necessary for long-distance overnight trains? They're not so difficult to get, but they'd want to see identity papers and God knows what, which is right out for the likes of us.'

Lomas looked crestfallen and Inga softened her criticism.

'No, the big trains are not for you and I, my dear. We must stick to the locals. We're both going to get heartily sick of trains and stations by the time we get to Moscow.'

'*Moscow!*' exclaimed Lomas. 'Surely that's one place–'

'How else are we going to get to Kiev? Look at that railway map over there. All lines go to Moscow from here. Anyway, my aunt there might be useful. There's an air service from Novosibirsk direct to Kiev, but aeroplanes, like express trains, are taboo. Anyway the police'll know by now your next port of call is Kiev. No doubt they'll soon be assembling your reception committee at Borispol Airport. No, look again. There's our train, the 09.40 to Cheremkhovo.'

'Never heard of it.'

'You will,' replied Inga cryptically as she walked over to the ticket hall.

The interior of the station was a seething mass of humanity. The waiting rooms, buffets and platforms were crammed. It was easy to get lost amongst the confusion and noise, so Lomas kept close to Inga, acknowledging her leadership. More to bolster his pride he attempted a further observation.

'Perhaps we ought to separate. They must know about you and will expect us to be together.'

'It's an idea. Yes, you're right. We'll meet on Platform 8 in fifteen minutes, that's 9.30 local time.' Inga checked her watch and wandered away into the crowds.

Immersing himself in a wall time-table, Lomas took stock of the position. That he had made a bit of a fool of himself in the hotel he was aware. But maybe Inga had not been so clever either. Perhaps he should have faced this police Johnny. He couldn't believe they had anything on him. Without a body, how could they? *Even* with a body for that matter. And now he and Inga had raised a hornet's nest. What were they going to do in Kiev? She seemed to expect salvation in the Ukranian capital. True he had a few friends in and around the city, but even if they were still there, even if they acknowledged him, what could they do? Bleak despair began to cloud the issues. He quickly switched his mind to Inga again. He had to admire the girl: she had guts and strength of character. Funny how she'd changed even within the few days he'd known her. At first she'd been submissive. Now, damn it, she was running the show. It was as if she knew the manner of her father's death. And suddenly the shaft of his thoughts struck home. *Why had she not only encouraged but led the escape from the hotel if she didn't believe that a crime had been committed?*

In a daze Lomas stumbled out on to the open platforms to find Inga waiting by an already full coach. The train left on time and they watched from a packed corridor the suburbs of Irkutsk disintegrate under pressure from the great Siberian forests. He found it difficult to reconcile the sweetly triumphant smile on Inga's lips with so ugly a word as blackmail.

It took five days to reach Novosibirsk. An endless succession of local trains jolted them through mile after mile of black *taiga,* rock infested with a thinning crust of cedar and aspen. Its terrible loneliness accentuated their predicament. The discomfort of the austere short-haul coaches, mostly crowded to suffocation with a tobacco and garlic-reeking peasantry, sapped their strength. Snatches of sleep at any hour of the day or night were small bonuses that could be found occasionally in wayside station waiting-rooms, open fields or on the train. Inga was the first to show the strain and it gave Lomas a grain of comfort to be able to exert once more a measure of male authority. They changed trains furtively, sneaking about the little wooden stations of Cheremkhovo, Kutulik, Tulin, Nizhne-Udinsk, Tayshet and Kansk, each one bearing its threat of danger. They were following the line of the Trans-Siberian Railway and each small township made the station its meeting hall, its market, the place where the action was. Consequently, authority kept its wary eye upon the platforms and the tracks, particularly when the big expresses came through. Unless their notoriety had reached the police stations of such lowly places, Inga's papers would pass scrutiny but Lomas's British passport – no longer backed by *Intourist* – was worse than useless. The kindly, simple-minded populace was quick to smell out strangers in their midst, so that each change of train became an ordeal.

Oddly, the sprawling city of Krasnoyarsk provided a semblance of security by virtue of its cosmopolitan atmosphere and big-town mentality. The couple managed a two-hour sleep in a cinema, and a decent meal, thus restoring their morale considerably. On the banks of the mile-wide Yenisei they became trippers as they joined the strollers in the park.

'If only Russian newspapers were as lurid as those of the West we might have learnt something.' Lomas had said, voicing both their anxieties.

'I doubt if even the finding of my poor father would warrant more than a local news item,' Inga had replied, appearing to miss the point, 'and likewise you dodging the clutches of *Intourist* is hardly headline stuff.'

Lomas had agreed, secretly wondering whether a murdered ex-KGB man wasn't the very elixir of any self-respecting newsman. But the basic question remained. Had a general call gone out to police divisions outside the district of Irkutsk?

From Krasnoyarsk the journey westwards had continued. Bogotol, Achinsk, Marunsk and Tajra became islands of treacherous communal warmth within a sea of ice-cold desolation. The dead flat countryside, suffused with a rash of trees that stretched into eternity, dulled the senses with its awful monotony and frightening distances. Occasional villages of mud and timber, peopled with hopeless men and women, loomed into sight, faded and were forgotten. Once a hint of strained-out mountains appeared in the far horizon, but the rise of land succumbed to the remorseless tundra.

Drawing into another city – Novosibirsk – was a relief. Novosibirsk has two stations: Novosibirsk One and Novosibirsk Two, the latter situated in the outer suburbs. For long afterwards Lomas was to chide himself for not alighting at the lesser station. It may not have made any difference, but the odds were that it would. The trouble was that both Lomas and Inga had convinced themselves of their anonymity.

Jumping down from a particularly hard hard-class coach, they negotiated the tracks to the station buildings and made for the exit. They saw the militiaman standing by the barrier, but fatigue dulled their senses.

'Papers,' he said, and held out a hand. An automatic rifle was slung, muzzle down, across his back.

Inga, after a moment of hesitation, offered her identity card. Lomas, stalling for time, made a show of looking for his. The passport would be a last resort. With Inga's card in his hand, the man consulted a list on the wall just inside his cabin. His excitement at the fact that the name on the identity card matched one of those on the wanted list was his undoing. By the time he had stepped forward to do his duty the couple were through, melting into the groups of people leaving the station. He yelled, ran a few yards, unslinging his weapon, then thought better of it and rushed back to the telephone in his cabin.

Their minds full of fright, Lomas and Inga broke into a fast walk upon the realization that they were not being pursued. Inga had lost her identity card but they had gained vital knowledge. Something had happened to transform them into hunted criminals.

An afternoon sun threw the shadows of cherry trees across the well-worn grass of the little park that lay a forgotten oasis within a complex of featureless buildings. The rumble of traffic, the intermittent screech and rattle of trams, made alien sounds in the untidy acre of nature planted and then neglected by man. Nobody was to accept its simple offering of peace that afternoon except a fugitive couple.

They had stumbled on it by accident. It seemed a good place in which to hold a council of war. They sat together on a broken seat, conscious of the solitude.

Lomas asked: 'With Novosibirsk Station out of the running, where do we go from here?'

Inga, looking haggard and older, spoke partly to herself. 'I wonder if we *could* make Moscow by air? Between us we're not short of funds.'

'I thought you said–'

'Yes, I did, but maybe I was exaggerating. The distance to Moscow is not so great as it is from Khabarovsk. They don't always ask for papers. It just depends.'

'On what?'

'Well, on the circumstances. It's not an external flight so one doesn't need passports and things like that, but for a 3000-mile journey they sometimes ask questions.'

To Lomas the idea of another series of train rides was equally abhorrent. The few hours the distance could be covered in a comfortable jet made it an enviable proposition.

'And what happens in Moscow?'

'I have an aunt there, as you know. She loves me deeply, thinks I'm wonderful and all that. I don't know if her love would stretch to harbouring us hardened criminals, but if we spin a pretty story she should be good for a day or two's rest.'

Lomas was silent for a moment, then made an abrupt switch of subject.

'That militiaman. He seemed to recognize your name. If so, why are they after you? Me, I can understand. I've absconded from *Intourist*, I've disobeyed the orders of a police officer and, and–' his voice faded.

Inga glanced at him sharply. 'Maybe they want me in connection with my father. His disappearance must be causing quite a stir back at home.'

'Yes, but you've committed no *crime*. They would only want to question you.'

Inga tossed her head with a sudden recharge of spirit. 'Listen, Lomas, I told you before, we're going to stick together in this right to the end. Obviously they've got us bracketed together, so we won't disappoint them.'

Lomas remembered the last time she had made this cryptic remark about sticking together to the end. It seemed a good time to settle the matter.

'What do you really expect to happen when we reach Kiev? I may have a few relations there, but they've no magic wands; they're not going to be able to mysteriously waft us through the border. I think you're labouring under a delusion.'

'Your relations; they're true Ukranians aren't they?'

'Yes, but that doesn't make them *that* much anti-Soviet. True, some were, but 20 years is a long time. They may have changed their attitudes. Even if not, I still don't see what they can do. You've put me in a position where I'm beginning to depend upon a few, maybe mystical, relations too, but I'm damned if I like it. Anyway, if they got us to Romania, what then? We'll still be hot numbers there.'

'I wasn't thinking of Romania.'

Lomas stared at Inga, a puzzled expression flickering across his face.

'Where then?'

'What's wrong with Turkey? We'd be okay there.'

'Turkey! That's miles from Kiev. I bet the border there is sealed tighter than a duck's arse.'

Inga winced at Lomas's involuntary description. He noticed the slight look of distaste and wondered how one who could be so brazen at sex was upset by a bawdy epithet.

'We shall have to see, won't we?' she said firmly.

The shadows in the park had grown

perceptively longer. It would be dark – and cold – before long.

'Let's go and see about that aeroplane,' she continued. 'If nothing else, the airport will be good for a night's sleep. Amongst the crowd there they'll never find us.'

With a certain amount of trepidation they caught a bus to the airport from the main square. At the big terminal buildings each hung back, watching for signs of a check on the incoming and outgoing crowds. The banshee wail of jets echoed against the modern concrete structure, but inside, beneath a high-pillared ceiling, the noise was muted by the babble of voices. Being no stranger to the airport, Inga led the way towards the ticket hall, pushing her way through the concentration of people.

'You wait there,' she commanded Lomas, indicating a corner. 'I'll deal with this.' She walked to a ticket window.

Lomas leaned against a pillar watching the girl move forward slowly in the short queue. He saw her speaking to an invisible being behind the glass and tried to determine the chances of success by her expression. But his attention was distracted. The feeling that someone was scrutinizing him from behind was a cold compress against the heart. He turned slowly and saw the expressionless little man pretending to be interested in a flight schedule. The Lenin-style cloth cap and badly fitting overcoat were features not lost upon Lomas. So they still had secret police 'narks' in the Soviet Union. He instinctively *knew* that's what he was. Way back in the early 1950s they were legion. A joker almost, but for the evil that made them tick. And then Lomas saw the companion. He stood a short distance away, a lean individual in a leather jacket, smoking a cigarette. Even as Lomas began to evalue their significance they closed in on him. The man in the overcoat reached him first.

'You will come with me, please,' he said, making no effort to explain his authority.

Lomas stared at him, his lip curling. He was quite calm. So it was the same old game, this surreptitious wielding of power by faceless, nameless parasites of a warped system. He was not really surprised. On the surface conditions in the USSR had improved, but he'd supposed it was too much to hope for a change in the basics. Now, he was being proved right and the knowledge produced only an irritation that he should have hoped otherwise.

The man's order was not worthy of a show

of indignation. Instead, Lomas took a deep breath and hit him in the stomach.

Even while he doubled up Lomas had grabbed Inga by the arm and was running with her towards the exit. They dodged round groups of people and mounds of luggage, knocked aside an airline official who made a half-hearted attempt to stop them, and sent spinning a small boy who blundered into their path. Exclamations of outrage arose behind them fanned into desultory pursuit by the colleague of the fallen man.

The couple reached the main entrance and ran out on to the wide tree-lined sweep of road. A parked row of taxis, their drivers in a huddle at the far end, caught Lomas's eye. There was little moving traffic.

They were close to the nearest taxi.

'Get in,' hissed Lomas, flinging himself into the driver's seat. He turned the ignition key but nothing happened. Several seconds were wasted fiddling with controls before he found the starter. At the second attempt the engine fired. To the accompaniment of a deplorable gear change and skidding tyres the old Ford Pilot slewed into the centre of the avenue. The shouts of the taxi drivers added to those of half a dozen men issuing from the terminal building.

Reaching the end of the airport road, Lomas steered left at the intersection.

Inga spoke for the first time.

'This is the way into the town. Surely–'

'No. We must get across the river. As soon as those two narks blow the gaff they'll close the bridges. It's obvious. The Ob's a natural. The railway bridge is permanently guarded anyway. Our only hope is the road.'

Inga saw his point. The River Ob was a formidable barrier. If they could make the bridge before the blocks went up it could give them valuable respite. The police would concentrate their attention on the east bank.

Lomas drove fast, establishing the feel of the car. They accelerated past a heavy lorry with a trailer and entered the city centre. The great parade ground of the main square, with the domed opera house to one side, gave him his bearings and, using it as a racecourse, overtook a double line of slow-moving vehicles. Someone blew a whistle but he ignored it. Trusting to his keen sense of direction, he turned into a two-carriageway avenue bearing due south.

Gradually the city deteriorated into a patchwork of unfinished buildings, broken kerbs and weed-infested pavements. From a roundabout they caught sight of the river and the steamer quays. Taking the most likely road the car closed in behind a slow-moving *Kvas** wagon and, horn blaring, drove it sulking on to the verge. To their right the great steel lattice sections snaked across the river. Up front the road bridge approaches lay unguarded. There was little traffic now and no sign of pursuit. A red banner raved *'Communism is Soviet power'* at them and they were on the western bank.

'We'll have to ditch this buggy first thing,' observed Lomas. 'It'll soon be red hot.' He slowed the car to a more respectable speed, not wishing to attract attention. A signpost whispered 'Kolyvan 103km.'

'There's a map here.' Inga was rummaging in the door pocket. She spread the sheet out and poured over it. 'Kolyvan's on the Moscow road but not the railway.'

'I think we'll give the railway a miss for a while,' said Lomas. 'I'm thinking we might make Omsk by road. There must be a fair amount of big stuff plying between Irkutsk and Moscow. Wish we could get to Kolyvan in this, but it's too much of a risk.'

Kvas, a supposedly non-alcoholic drink made from bread.

The west bank suburbs of Novosibirsk were little more than a shanty town and soon petered out. The great forests of birch and larch – a scintillating curtain of gold and silver in the dying sun – closed in to jostle the road grudging even the narrow strip of tarmac that ran straight as an arrow through their concentrated ranks.

About ten miles out of the city an unsign-posted by-road led the old Ford deep into the trees. The surface became progressively worse until it was all but impassable. Bumping over muddy cart-tracks, Lomas turned the car into the pin-cushion of trunks and ran on until the wheels became firmly entrenched in the soft earth. He cut the engine.

Inga shivered slightly. Though the day had been warm the chill of winter was invading the autumn nights. In the course of a few hours the temperature would plummet to zero.

'Let's stay in the car till morning.'

'I think you're right,' replied Lomas. 'Even if we got a lift we'd probably be pitchforked out somewhere in the back of beyond.'

He climbed from the car and explored the contents of the boot. It produced a thread-bare rug that had obviously been used for covering the radiator.

'No double beds in stock I'm afraid, but this'll be better than nothing.' Lomas brandished aloft his find. Following a voyage of exploration in the vicinity of the car, they settled down supperless to sleep. Fatigue would help them overcome the cold and the hunger and they would be up with the dawn dependent upon the luck of the road for the onward journey. A stagnant pool in a moss-covered dip would serve their ablutions. Lomas thanked God for remembering to stuff a razor and soap into his pocket. At least they had the means of keeping reasonably clean.

A great silence descended with the darkness.

CHAPTER ELEVEN

The view over the rooftops to the mighty Amur from his third-floor office was usually calculated to relieve the tensions of Colonel Spassky. Its solemn splendour, the calm, unhurried progress of its waters, were a balm to a seething mind, a burdened brain. In the face of such giant forces the petty tribulations of men took on their true perspective. But not today. For the first time the panorama produced only exasperation. The river, damn it, was mocking him.

Spassky turned savagely away. It was a black week in his career. It had started, he supposed, with the absconding of the pseudo-Englishman Lomas from his Irkutsk hotel. Then the double evasion of arrest by him and Igor's girl in Novosibirsk. Damned clumsy police work but nothing much in that as far as he, Spassky was concerned. It was only a matter of time. No, it was the new development that mattered. Only yesterday he had remembered the taped transcript of the criminal Marchenko's rigged trial. There were few copies about and they carried a high security classification. They were being circulated to a limited number of KGB officers as an example of a technique the Soviet leadership wanted re-established for dealing with the latest eruption of the Jewry. A carefully rigged sentence here and there resulting in a ten-year sentence would make them think. Their pathetic protests were giving the Soviet Union a bad name throughout the world, but it would be nothing to what that confounded tape could do if it got into the wrong hands. He didn't approve of the sombre return to the Stalin methods, but he saw the reasoning. This wasn't the point, however. He had lent the tape to Igor and, with Igor, it had disappeared. He'd been a fool, he could see that now, but Igor had been involved in parts of the Marchenko trial and was curious. Igor wasn't amongst the selected few ordered to make a study of the tape, but he was KGB, one of the family so to speak, and there seemed no harm in lending it. Poor Igor had been found floating in that damned river out there, but the tape was nowhere to be found.

All day Spassky had spent making a personal search of the Reprostovich flat. He hadn't dared designate the task. Anyway, he'd made the fool of himself so it was up to him alone to put the matter right. But the tape wasn't in the flat. Of that he was certain. Discreet enquiries had been made at Igor's office. No, Comrade Reprostovich had put nothing in the safe; his confidential secretary could vouch for the fact personally. So? There could be but one direction he could look! The girl, Inga. She must have it. And if she did there must be a reason. And, to Spassky, the reason smelt of treason.

He could wait until nightfall before he gave the alarm. They would break him for it, he supposed. Incidents in his life rose unbidden to cloud the issue, but he swept them away. He mustn't get morbid about things. He'd made one mistake and in his job it was one mistake too many. He must not shirk his duty.

So they'd lost the couple at Novosibirsk airport. The criminal police were scouring the town east of the river. They didn't think they'd had time to reach the bridges before they'd sealed them. They were watching the ferry-crossing points and the places where the small boats lay up.

Spassky watched the phones on his desk. They remained sternly silent. He knew

Novosibirsk would be on the moment of any new development. He knew in his heart that the fugitives had managed to cross the river. It was going to be more than a criminal matter now. The political boys were going to love him.

The Amur had faded into the gloom of evening. A chill draught knifed in from the window. Resignedly Spassky reached for the furthest telephone and asked for a line to Moscow.

CHAPTER TWELVE

Aleksandr Biryuzov drove his articulator with skilful abandon. He made the Gorky-Moscow run every week, so that his boast of knowing each pot-hole in the route was no idle one. A Ukranian of 28, he took life with a minimum of seriousness; continuously flouting authority while keeping precariously within the law. The trait was reflected not only in his driving but also in his appearance. A mop of long hair which he fondly imagined to resemble that of Tom Jones, his doyen of the Western world, hung limply over his shoulders. Centred within the tangle was a mobile face creased with either scorn or laughter, for he had little use for other emotions. But the flag of his revolt to Soviet society was his attire. A startling check suit, velvet collared and exaggeratingly drain-piped, offered a uniformity with the British 'spiv' era of the 1950s.

But Aleksandr Biryusov's revolt went deeper than that. A native of Kremenchug, he exalted in his exile to a Moscow transport agency and brandished his Ukrainian upbringing at anyone who was either enthusiastically Russian or had raised a voice against his country. He was, however, in a more docile mood that morning. The couple he'd picked up near Vladimir had given him food for thought. He'd instantly recognised in Lomas a fellow Ukrainian and after the back-slapping they'd chatted about their respective home towns. It became painfully obvious to Aleksandr that his fellow country-man hadn't been to Kiev for at least a decade. Quite obviously too the bloke and his 'skirt' were in trouble. Yet they weren't 'professionals', otherwise they wouldn't have shown it so easily. He'd been on the road too long, had Aleksandr, not to recognize the symptoms of those who travelled the roads with him.

Typically, he had come straight to the point.

'How long have they been after you?'

Both Lomas and Inga feigned surprise at the question and attempted explanations. Even without the waves of fatigue that engulfed them, both saw they couldn't pull a fast one over their new companion.

'Okay, you win,' said Lomas resignedly. 'It's the politicals. If you think we're too hot you'd better put us down.'

A vast smile crossed Aleksandr's face. He stamped hard on the accelerator and the truck leaped forward. No one ever asks your 'crime' if the 'politicals' are involved. You either protect the guy with your life or drop him like a brick. With a fellow Ukrainian on the hot seat Aleksandr's course of action was clear.

'You really want to go Moscow?'

Lomas hesitated before replying. There was Inga's aunt who, if reliable, could give them a bolt-hole for a day or two. Otherwise the Soviet capital held nothing for them. He realized that the mythical bolt-hole there was as uncertain as those likely to be found in his own home town. It was just that Moscow was nearer.

'No, it happens to be on the way to Kiev.'

Inga entered the conversation.

'What about Tatiana? Aren't we going to lie up there?' she said in a tired voice. 'Tatiana is a relative,' she added in an aside to the driver.

Aleksandr was brutal with his reply.

'If the politicals are after you they'll have her on a string. Better go nowhere near the place. We'll be at the city road check in a couple of hours. They'll be there, too, if you're as hot as I think you are.'

'We're hot enough,' confirmed Lomas dryly.

'Well, what *do* you suggest?' Inga spoke with a trace of irritation, seeing the demise of a comfortable refuge.

The smile still puckered Aleksandr's face. 'Maybe I could take you to Kiev.'

Lomas and Inga looked at the young Ukrainian with amazement. It sounded too good to be true. Lomas tried to keep the eagerness out of his voice.

'Why should you? It's a hell of a way. How will you explain it to your outfit? No, surely you need only get us on the Kiev road.'

'Take first things first. Can you drive?'

'Yes.'

'We can make Kiev within 24 hours if we keep going and you can relieve me for a couple of hours. Got any money?'

'Plenty. As much as you want.'

A cloud momentarily crossed Aleksandr's face. 'Not for *me* comrade, just for the juice. My outfit, as you call it, only gives me petrol coupons for the regular run.'

Lomas accepted the reprimand in silence. He realized he'd been too long out of Russia.

'How will you square this unauthorized

little excursion with your boss?'

Aleksandr tossed his curls contemptuously. 'I can twist those Russian fools round my finger. A breakdown, sickness, I could even say you forced me to make the trip if it came to it. But they won't be sweating about me for a day or two. My cargo's low priority. It's been hanging around for weeks. Anyway, that's my worry, not yours.'

The township of Noginsk passed by in a litter of untidy buildings and dust. The road began to improve for the straight run into Moscow. Evening was reflected in the flat grey country broken here and there by a sprinkling of trees standing out like bristles on a badly shaved chin. Lomas and Inga lay against each other, lulled into half-sleep by the warmth of the cab and the steady throb of the engine. Both of them had lost count of the number of lorries they'd ridden since that early morning van had picked them up on the road to Kolyvan. There, on the main expressway – a vital artery across Siberia – the onward journey had been assured. Long-distance transport plied the route and the fraternity of the road was strong. Nights had been spent in warm lorry cabs or draughty trucks, their immediate future entrusted to nameless drivers. One night had been passed in the musty hay of a barn and for another they had been invited into a tiny smoke-filled *Izba,* there to share a mattress on the floor.

Aleksandr began to hum a Ukrainian love song and the only indication the couple had that they had turned off the main road was a worsening of the road surface compensated for by a slight slackening of speed.

'We'll hit the expressway to Tula in about three hours,' announced Aleksandr to nobody in particular.

Lomas and Inga heard him as through a wall of cotton wool. Even as slumber closed their minds both realized how lucky they had been so far. And Aleksandr had been the biggest break of all.

The Dnieper at Kiev is proportionate to the size of the city, neither dwarfing it like the Amur does to Khabarovsk or allowing itself to detract from the elegance of the capital city of the Ukraine. Kiev itself lies on the high western bank of the river and is linked by a single road bridge to the fast-growing suburbs of Darnitsa and Poznyaki. It was in Darnitsa that Lomas was born, though he failed entirely to match up the cubic wilderness of concrete it now was with the little village where he had spent his early life.

As Aleksandr drove the big lorry slowly across the bridge, Lomas's eyes flicked over the expanse of factories and multiple-storey flats, seeking a tiny fragment of recognition. Inga watched him anxiously. They came to the southern parapet and Alexsandr said, 'Left, right or straight on?'

'Right,' replied Lomas on impulse. At least the river hadn't changed. He suddenly remembered making mud dams wherever streams entered the river upstream of the bridge.

The truck swung in a tight turn to fill the whole of the side road that led them along the river bank. A quarter of a mile they crawled before the road petered out into a rash of back gardens and waste ground.

'My home stood back 300 yards or so from around here,' said Lomas, his eyes darting everywhere, 'but there's nothing left I can recognize, nothing at all. I can only judge it to be about here by the distance from the bridge. It's hopeless.' The excitement in his voice drained away.

Inga put in a suggestion. 'The river bank itself surely that hasn't changed?'

Lomas walked to the water's edge and

stared vaguely about him. 'In twenty years water does things to earth and soil. You don't notice it at the time, only like now. All the little indents where I played and fished have changed their shape.'

He became aware that people were staring at them from the surrounding dwellings. A bunch of children had come through a gap in the hedge to stand with curiosity stamped in eyes that were sullen and suspicious. Aleksandr noticed it, too, and motioned the couple back to the cab.

'They'll have the law on us soon,' he muttered.

With ponderous deliberation the truck made an elephantine waltz as a prelude to returning the way it had come. Aleksandr manipulated the gears like a man conducting an orchestra. Lomas sensed his nervousness.

'Look, Alex,' he said, 'we can go our own way now. You've been wonderful to us and we can never thank you enough for what you've done. But I'm on home ground now even if–' He made a gesture and shrugged.

'If you go around looking for relatives you'll end up underground,' growled Aleksandr, annoyed that his nervousness had shown. 'What applied in Moscow for your girl friend equally applies to you here.

Haven't either of you got any nice unrelated friends?'

'He's right,' put in Inga, 'we're asking for trouble looking for anyone they can connect with you and I.'

'Drop up here,' Lomas commanded, 'before we get to the main road. This thing'll start getting conspicuous if we use it to explore the town.'

Aleksandr did as he was bid. He gave Lomas a great bear hug and Inga the politest of kisses. No words passed between them, but the atmosphere was charged with emotion.

The truck lumbered off down the road leaving the couple staring after it. They were going to miss the warmth of the friendly cab. It made it all the more unpleasant to face the cold again.

Because of a faulty distributor and subsequent decision to lay up the second night, they had made Kiev at first light. This gave a full day to make contact before nightfall. What they would do if this deadline wasn't met gnawed at their vitals. Lomas supposed they would have to take to the country again for a place to sleep since by hanging around in a built-up area was asking to be picked up. Inga shied away from thinking about it at all, content to give Lomas his head. It was his city and his problem. After all, if it came to it, he was the one they were after.

Lomas still found it difficult to believe that his notoriety could have spread as far as Kiev whatever the police may have found to pin on him. Certainly not as a runaway tourist, though there was the matter of his *Intourist* itinerary which, together with his birth records, must point to Kiev. Uncertain of themselves, seeing policeman in every passer-by, the couple recrossed the bridge.

At least the city centre hadn't changed. Damn it, the place looked younger and fresher than it had in the days of his youth. Then he remembered. Of course, they'd rebuilt the place, brick by brick, as it had looked before the war. The Khreshchetik – the main street – gave off the same expansive air as it had when he was a child. The impressive conformity of its façade still frightened him, though the ranks of lime and poplar trees accompanying an exaggerated roadway softened the majestic lines. Behind the Khreshchetik the couple tried to lose themselves in the back streets. But there are no back streets, or at least very few, in Kiev. It is a city where every nook and cranny can look you squarely in the eye and just when you think you're reaching a quiet, forgotten corner an enormous bubble-domed church or cathedral rears its lofty head. It is disconcerting to anyone, but to Lomas and Inga came a perception akin to walking naked into the Albert Hall.

But its sameness lent them one advantage. Lomas knew where he was going. His step was purposeful.

'Is this Andrei Zenkevich quite reliable?' Inga asked for the second time.

Lomas did not like the inference behind the question. Andrei was the best friend he ever had. At least he was when they were both in their 'teens. Yet he knew she was right to be suspicious. What life and politics had done to him was anybody's guess.

'Are *you* reliable?' he responded bitterly.

They came to a district close to the railway station. The sound of trains echoed against the heavy buildings.

'It's number 14 up the road.' Excitement was back in Lomas's voice.

The street was bordered by a mixture of large wooden *Izba*'s and four-storey plaster-faced apartment blocks. Few people were in evidence and in spite of its width was the nearest Kiev could get to a backstreet.

139

Number 14 was on the ground floor of one of the blocks. Their ring was answered by a hard-faced woman exhibiting a formidable range of toothless gums.

'Does Comrade Zenkevich still live here?' enquired Lomas.

The gums remained clamped until the gimlet eyes had surveyed the young couple. Curiosity overcame suspicion.

'Why do you want to know?' she croaked.

'I'm an old friend of his. We've come a long way to see him.'

The woman saw she was going to get no more information. 'He left twelve years ago.'

'Do you know where he went?'

'No.'

Lomas understood that even had she known, she wasn't telling. They moved up to a stone stairway to the first floor. Lomas selected a door a short way along the corridor simply because it wore a fresh coat of paint and therefore looked the more inviting. A middle-aged man answered their knock.

'Yes, I know your friend,' he replied in response to Lomas's question. 'He moved the other side of town, oh, it must be more than ten years ago.'

'You don't happen to know which street?'

'No, but it's hard against St Sofia's. You

could make enquiries there.'

They both thanked the man and returned to the street. Again they traversed the city, moving with the afternoon crowds that thronged the multiple pavements and arcades of the Khreshchetik. In Kalinin Square an abnormal number of policemen hung about but not with a particularly purposeful air. Alarmed the couple shied away until Lomas remembered that extra police had always been on duty in the square as a sort of throwback to the 1905 revolution.

The cathedral of St Sophia was not hard to locate. Its golden domes, painstakingly restored, made a landmark in the city. No longer classed as a house of God, it nevertheless drew a steady clientele whose interest in religious relics was but a vehicle for silent prayer. Lomas and Inga joined the throng to stand a moment beneath the golden ikons and painted effigies. Nearby an old gnarled peasant woman and a *tolstofka*-clad man prayed defiantly before an altar that was exhibit Number 427 in the official catalogue. A barely perceptible chant rose and fell like the sighing of the wind.

Inga stood transfixed, her eyes fastened upon the old peasants and others surreptitiously worshipping between the pillars and walls of vivid Byzantine mosaic. The atmosphere was heady with an emotion stronger than incense. Lomas watched her from behind a statue, abruptly conscious of a new, almost classical beauty in the girl whose destiny he controlled. Beyond the tiredness in her eyes, the travel-worn clothes, the unkemptness of her hair, he saw a woman of striking appearance, standing erect, dignified and proud, able to scorn her persecutors and exhibit the sort of courage rare in her sex. 'Backbone,' 'moral fibre,' that's what the English called it. That's what Inga had. But in addition to these attributes she had a humility that touched her heart and reassured him. There had been moments when he had wondered about her. Moments when as if a cold hand – cold as the permafrost of Siberia – had come between them. There had even been that moment he had imagined she might be using him. How silly it sounded. Look at her now, revelling in the beauty of the surroundings, a true Russian woman proud of her country but not impervious to the emotions that religion can stir in the basest of human hearts.

But even as he watched there came a transformation that sent a blizzard raging where a moment ago the spark of love burnt fierce. Inga's finely chiselled features drew taut, a mask he had never seen before stole across her face to twist the mouth into a grimace of scorn and revulsion that was hardly human in its hate.

Lomas's reaction brought with it its own reactions. His emotions were not clear cut, which they usually were, his rational mind would normally sort the components of any experience neatly into mental boxes, he would deal with the most important, which resulted in the discarding of the rest. Now, the affection, his own cautious word for his feelings for Inga, his fatigue, the restriction of movement and freedom to act as he would wish, and the impact of his immediate surroundings drained his reasoning power; the situation would not respond to his usual mental processing. His first reaction was one of dismay at the thought that Inga's scorn was for him, feeling as he did towards her, then he was perplexed, then worried almost to panic because of his puzzlement. For an instant he felt himself to be a total and complete stranger hovering on the edge of human relations, totally alone. Inga's relaxing features dispelled his mental tangle.

Inga had caught the near anguish in his features, realizing that it mirrored an anguish that must be in her own face. But her anguish was a different emotion however, born of the will to survive as the person she wished to be, the person she clung to in the face of many an inner argument, her wilful, arrogant, tenacious self always winning. Lomas – or rather his presence and his plans – had gained an ally in the very surroundings in which they stood; the grandeur, purpose, achievement, seemed to swell the character of this stranger who was fast losing his strangeness, denting the armour that protected her against the fact that he was dependent upon her. She had hoped that, through Lomas, she could shuffle off her father's dependence, but found that Lomas the antidote was turning into the original poison.

The dramatic atmosphere of the cathedral touched her with its whisperings of selflessness. She hit back in a vehement survival protest; she was human, a unique human being, not needing this theatrical nonsense to bolster her. The conflict pulled tight her face muscles, tugging away the dignity that her convictions gave it.

At that moment she caught Lomas's eye. For an instant she felt ashamed and guilty, and she relaxed her features. Then she felt sad for herself, sad that she had compromised. Hard on this thought came the reluctant reasoning that she must be prepared to compromise in order to hold on to her independent, unassailable soul! She quickly changed the thought word for self and smiled suddenly, easily, at the slip.

It had all happened so quickly, in so ethereal a manner that Lomas found it expedient to put it down to a moment of madness, an overdrawn imagination and to the changed atmosphere of the great church. Surely such a place was more susceptible to miracles than to evil spells.

Less than five minutes later Lomas got his miracle. They were leaving the building when a voice from behind, shrill with astonishment, rang through the hushed assembly.

'Ilyich! Ilyich Palatnik and surely no other!'

Lomas and Inga whirled, fear and surprise showing momentarily in their faces.

Lomas was the first to recover. All the years that had passed could not obliterate the rugged features of Andrei Zenkevich. Here, surely, was the second stroke of good fortune. Just one more and the ordeal could be over.

It never occurred to Lomas to hide anything from Andrei; anything, that is, that Inga herself didn't know. In spite of the twenty-year interval their friendship simply continued from the point it had been broken. For both of them it could not have been otherwise.

Talking animatedly, the two men, with a bewildered Inga trailing behind, trooped out of the cathedral, crossed the paved surround and let themselves into one of a small group of *Izba* houses dwarfed by a big block rising from where neighbouring *Izba*'s had once been. Andrei's wife, Nina, young and timid, was hurriedly introduced then banished to the kitchen to prepare a meal.

'How long have you been married, you old bluebeard,' asked Lomas jovially.

'Only a couple of years,' replied Andrei. 'I successfully avoided it until then. But maybe you're about to put your own head in the noose.'

They both looked at Inga as a prize Shorthorn. She felt a flush of embarrassment infuse her cheeks. Lomas saved her from the necessity of a retort.

'There'll be no wedding bells for us whilst we are in this country,' he put in, 'so if you want to see me similarly fettered you'll have to help us get out.'

The remark was couched as a joke, but Andrei caught the underlay of seriousness behind it. His grinning face shadowed slightly.

'We'll discuss the matter after a meal,' he said, and relapsed into a catalogue of reminiscences.

Though Ukrainian to the core, Andrei had none of his countrymen's visual attributes. He was tall and thin, his clothes hung on him and, though only a year older than Lomas, his head showed unmistakable signs of balding. Otherwise it was a handsome head and the face held both compassion and intelligence. In spite of an obvious joy at meeting the friend of his youth there was a nervous rapidity in his actions. Purely by accident, in that the police records were inaccurately compiled, Andrei had escaped the fate of Lomas at the war's end. Instead he had gone on to study aeronautical engineering at Kiev University and now ran the airframe design department in an aircraft component factory at Darnitsa.

Aeroplanes and Andrei had been inseparable, as had once been Andrei and Lomas. When the human partnership had been broken by Lomas's arrest Andrei had turned his full attention to aeroplanes. He did well at his studies; too well, in fact, for his knowledge of design had kept him firmly on the ground, the State seeing in him more value as an architect than a flyer. Disappointed at missing a chance to become a pilot in the war because of his lack of years and the German occupation, he had joined the DAAF⋆ and spent most of his free hours contentedly aloft. Nina had objected once to his neglect of her, but only once. That one demonstration had nearly severed the marriage, and ever since she had resigned herself to taking second place in her husband's heart.

Nina herself was something of an enigma. She was a Georgian, a native of Tbilisi, with the quickfire temper of her breed. But she had accepted the insult of her husband's first love as if it were a part of life that was unchangeable. In lesser things Andrei gave way to her few demands. That way he attained his freedom to fly without unpleasantness. In appearance she was anaemic-looking, her dead-white skin accentuated by long straight hair. A delicate health had been

⋆The Soviet equivalent of an association of aero clubs. As might be expected, it is a para military organisation.

a cross to bear all her life and she had never ceased to wonder at having being a catch for any man, particularly a man the calibre of Andrei. It was her one break in life.

The smell of cooking permeated the old house. To Lomas and Inga it was a delight. For days they had been eating where and what they could in lorry drivers' restaurants and snack bars. Now, in warm comfort, they could relax and enjoy a meal once more. And the promise was as good as its smell. A thick vegetable soup and a roast crowned with sour cream sauce washed down by a fine Georgian red wine. In spite of short notice, Nina could always be relied upon never to let down her husband and his guests.

It was Nina who had refused to move into one of the superior apartments that were springing up around them. Not only was their *Izba* more spacious, but its old-fashioned homeliness was fast becoming the envy of those who lived in modern 'luxury' – clinical and standardized – on their very doorstep. As she animatedly explained to Inga over coffee, it was warmer, too.

'They freeze up there you know. It can be just as cold here as from where you come, and there's always something not working in the central-heating system as, no doubt, you know.' Maybe she had noticed Inga's disapproving glances at the antiquity of the big living-room with its heavy dark furniture, the rocking chair, generations of family photographs and the porcelain stove with its flue pipe snaking across the ceiling. At any rate, she took pains to ensure that their choice of unprogressive living was not laid at the door of Andrei's ability or lack of it.

With the meal cleared away and both women at their respective tasks – Nina's in the kitchen, Inga's in the bathroom – the two men sank back into fireside chairs. Andrei smoked a black cheroot as he led the conversation back to the subject of his heart's desire.

'What flying have you managed during your sojourn in the capitalistic world?' he asked without a trace of sarcasm.

'Precious little,' Lomas answered. 'Not all is gold, as one is expected to believe of the West. Few people indeed are millionaires and to fly seriously in Britain you've got to be just that.'

'Did you manage any?'

'I became an associate member of a Surrey aero club for a while, but it was more drinking than flying. Those who had their own machines were all right, but for the rest it was a case of exerting influence over the operations secretary. Oh, I managed a few trips, but then they raised the sub and I backed out.'

'Here things are different. Much better, too, than when we were young. They *encourage* you to fly here if you have the slightest ability. Money doesn't come into it. I suppose that's where the two systems come apart.'

Lomas looked sharply at his friend. This didn't sound quite like the old Andrei he knew. Once they had both been rebels; admittedly more against authority in general than any authority in particular, but rebels all the same. Of course, living in the Soviet Union one couldn't go on rebelling for ever, but Andrei's taut little speech smelt of surrender.

Andrei sensed Lomas's suspicion. He grinned sheepishly.

'I was talking in the context of flying,' he said. 'Like you, I'm a Ukrainian and shall never willingly accept the Soviet system. But my one accomplishment has given me a reasonable job and opportunity to indulge in my favourite pastime. I even belong to the Party' – he lifted his chin in mock challenge – 'not because I believe in it, but because it helps me in the things I want to do.'

'Do you go flying every weekend?'

'Generally – yes.'

'Can you go anywhere you like?' Suddenly it was Lomas asking the questions.

'Within the borders, of course, and excluding military zones. I wish you could come on a flight with me. It'd be like old times.'

There was more than mock challenge in Lomas's reply.

'I will, Andrei, I will. It's how you're getting us out of this damned country of yours.'

CHAPTER THIRTEEN

The ordeal had not been so bad as he had expected. They'd not relieved him of his command or his post, instead they'd said get the tape back and they would reconsider his indiscretion in the light of its safe return.

Colonel Spassky was very satisfied with the turn of events. He'd been given full charge of the operation both from a political and criminal angle and had moved to Police Headquarters at Novosibirsk to be closer to the scene of the hunt. As far as the criminal boys were concerned, it was entirely a criminal matter and he'd felt no need to mention the other thing. When they'd brought in poor Igor it was this Lomas fellow he'd suspected of the crime but with the disappearance of the tape he wasn't so sure. Igor's daughter could have had a hand in it, a theory that was given strength by their combined evasion of authority in this very city a week ago.

They'd drawn a blank in Moscow. Igor's sister had been discreetly watched from the beginning and new arrivals into the capital checked. Of course, nothing could be certain, but he'd put his money on Kiev. It was Lomas's birthplace, the fellow had relatives and probably friends there and must know the place pretty well. It would have been where he – Spassky – would have gone had he been a fugitive in the USSR. True, Lomas must be aware of the deduction, but still Spassky's faith remained unshaken. Those canny Ukrainians would give him a hiding place for sure. That's where the couple would be.

A watch on the Palatnik relatives had, of course, been executed, but had produced no results. He didn't think it would. Still, he'd centred his forces upon Kiev, firm in his convictions. Calmly he waited.

Then had come the slice of luck he'd been expecting. Outside Chernigov a road patrol had picked up a lorry driver for speeding. His papers showed him to be hundreds of miles off course. The explanations had not rung true and they had held the man while the incident was reported to police HQ at Gomel. They would probably have let him go had not, by chance, Kiev Command got wind of the report and a further interrogation of the driver instigated.

Finally, the fellow had broken down and Spassky himself had interviewed the frightened man.

Spassky's intuition had been proved right. Kiev it was.

CHAPTER FOURTEEN

Ever since their flight from Novosibirsk the question mark of escape from the Soviet Union had lain like a canker upon the mind of Lomas. Few people had accomplished the project. Most of the hermetically-sealed borders led only to other Communist states, where the whole process of escape would have to begin again in lands where both he and Inga would be the more conspicuous. Only Turkey could offer a solution on that score, though the rugged and hostile mountains of Armenia would see to it that the solution was no simple one. But detailed planning could not begin until contacts had been made, for inside help would be a vital ingredient to any plan. The chance meeting with Andrei had brought him one step nearer, but it was only while his friend had been enthusing about his aeronautical prowess that a method presented itself.

There was nothing new about escape by aeroplane, nor had there been found much new in the way of a remedy. Interceptor aircraft were too fast, radar of little use so long as the target hugged the ground. No, the safeguards would doubtless be wrapped up less dramatically in the preliminaries, which made it all the more necessary to have the co-operation of a trusted friend who knew the ropes and could wield some authority.

Needless to say, Andrei had been horrified by Lomas's declaration. At first he'd taken it as a joke and weaved a fantasy around the actions to be taken. Then he stopped laughing when he saw that his sarcasm was being taken at its face value.

'But you haven't got a pilot's licence,' he'd finally objected.

'What's that matter? I can fly, as you well know. I'm probably a bit rusty, but no doubt you can take me up on dual control for an initial spin. Where is your base anyway?'

'Out near Borispol. It adjoins the airport.'

'What sort of machines have you got?'

'Jak's mostly. Plus a few Czech Aero 45s. Better than those old captured Storches we used to use.'

Lomas smiled. He remembered the Storches. If you could fly them you could fly anything.

'What's their range?'

'The Jak's you mean. Oh, about 500 kilometres.'

Lomas brought out a battered map and paced his fingers across the outspread sheet.

'Odessa's about 260 from here. Miles I mean. Then there's another 345 across the Black Sea.'

Andrei frowned over Lomas's shoulder.

'It can't be done. Whoever heard of a Jak doing 1000 kilometres in one hop!'

'Who said anything about one hop?' Hasn't Odessa got a DAAF base, or even Sevastopol?' Lomas exhibited excitement. 'And look, Sevastopol is only 300 kilometres from Turkish territory. Surely, there are no difficulties in refuelling on bases other than your own?'

Andrei admitted that there weren't. 'But you have to make prior application,' he countered. He saw the thing was running away from him. 'And you've overlooked something else.'

'What?'

'Look at that Turkish land mass. It's all mountain and rock. Not even a gnat could put down there. The only flat is around Istanbul and Adapazari.'

Lomas snorted. 'You're just looking for trouble. I'd land on the beach if necessary.

Anywhere along that coast. I'm not doing this for fun you know.'

'You don't expect me to come with you on this mad caper do you?'

'Glory be, no, though it *would* be rather like old times! It seems to me the fewer bodies to be carried the better if we're not going to run out of juice. I'll just "borrow" a machine when you're sort of not looking and we'll be away. No doubt the Turks will return it in due course.'

Andrei shook his head in disbelief. It had always been like that. Whenever he and Ilyich had got together it had spelt trouble. But in those days it was different. He was now a respectable citizen and he wanted it to stay that way.

Lomas was waffling on; weaving fantasies of his own from the map.

'Of course we could cut out the Black Sea altogether if we took off for the final flight from Armenia to Georgia. It's a land border there even if it does mean getting up to 17,000 to cross the confounded mountains. Nina lives that way, too, which could be useful. Incidentally, what's the ceiling of these Jak crates?'

It was at that moment that Nina came back into the room. Her face was whiter than usual. Outside dusk was shadowing the streets.

'Nina, what's wrong?' Andrei hurried over to his wife.

'It's your friends,' she whispered huskily. 'The police are all over town looking for them. I just stepped out to get more bread and meat and I was stopped twice. They asked if I had seen them. They even know their names.'

'Did they say why they're after them?'

Nina's eyes grew big.

'For murder!' she said.

Andrei turned to Lomas, enquiry inscribed across his face.

Lomas returned the gaze calmly. So they'd found Kunetsov. Well, even if they had, they couldn't prove he'd been murdered. Their headlong flight from Irkutsk hadn't helped any, but the charge could only be based upon supposition. Murder surely wasn't going to turn the whole Soviet Union into a tizzy. What else had the authorities got on them?

His baffled features were misinterpreted by Andrei. A new respect came into his voice.

'We'll have to get you out of this place fast,' he said. 'I'll book a Jak for tomorrow.'

Andrei went to work with a will. Much as he was pleased to see Ilyich back from the dead as it were, the urge to get rid of him and his girl friend was stronger. They were unhealthy people to have around. That they had turned up on a Sunday was a stroke of luck; that he'd chosen not to go flying that day simply because of a sore throat was another. A telephone call to his office settled his absence from work for a couple of days. Another reserved him a dual-control Jak for two hours in the morning. He had a long chat with the duty officer about a mythical long-distance flight he felt he might have to make and got the chap to indent for the various requirements that would have to be fulfilled at a number of bases in the south. It was hardly possible to cover every contingency at such short notice, but he felt confident at being able to play by ear anything else that might arise. The first day would be a dry run wherein he would put Ilyich through his paces and get the base people used to the sight of him. On the second Ilyich and Inga would be on their own.

All four of them had gone to bed early that Sunday night. Lomas and Inga were tired; Andrei and Nina tense and exhausted by the day's events. Beneath his big double bolster Lomas tossed spasmodically, unable to sleep as excitement coursed through his mind. Here at last was a plan, a method that offered hope where previously there had been nothing but a despairing vacuum. To combat the excitement he forced his mind to explore the delicious possibilities of success, of life with a beautiful girl and of an existence that would be for ever enhanced by the memory of a great experience. But the knife edge of excitement, backed by drumbeats of rising terror, kept returning to stir the tide of contentment.

Inga, too, lay sleepless, staring into a darkness full of the reflections of her thoughts. Just ahead lay the goal that for years she had considered unattainable. To live in the West had been a dream that had haunted her since the austere period of her teenage years. Not that what the West called 'freedom' and the load of old guff it put about concerning the right to free speech, free religion and all that meant much to her. But in the West one could live without the State breathing down your neck. It was a place where to be rich was no crime, where it was possible to live as one desired and not to pre-set patterns concocted by faceless old men crazed with the creed of Socialism. In Lomas she had found her chance and seized it. She had seen in him a man who knew what he was after, a man of purpose, and she had been right. Hadn't he severed the chain that bound her to her father and brought her now to the very threshold of that goal? That he would accomplish the final act of her liberation she had little doubt. Of the man himself she had more. But at least he was a man, which was something. She even liked him in spite of his inability to attain her fullest aspirations. As if actuated by a switch, her mind sprang from the future back into the present. Against the mighty opposition of the whole USSR could they manage it?

Even passive opposition would have been a formidable obstacle, but the new development wherein the police of the whole country were actively bent upon their apprehension was a frightening one. But why? The question once more flung itself upon the threshold of her deliberations. Except for consorting with a renegade tourist she had committed no crime however you looked at it. The knowledge offered comfort. Even if her father's body had been found she could see no reason for the universal interest of the police – unless, of course... Inga wrestled with a new idea and frightened herself into near panic. For comfort she crept into Lomas's room next door.

Lomas half expected her. In a way he was glad of her company in his bed as a diversion for his own crazed meanderings. He found himself studying anew his feelings for this Russian Jewess who was this moment working herself into a sexual frenzy by his side. Abruptly he was quite calm, detached even. He could feel the vibrations of her body and hear the low moans that escaped her as she willed him to move in on her to hurt her, to give himself to her. His calmness was antagonizing her; he knew it and he held it deliberately as he thought of her as his wife, as the bearer of his children, as an expensive luxury demanding much and giving little except her body, and perhaps not even that as new men with money came into her life. He remembered her words, 'I've got you for better or for worse.' Maybe it was simply the deliberation of a determined woman, but could it be more? Did she know the truth about her father? Had his removal been her intention all along? Was he simply a tool of her evil genius? His mind became a dirt track of whirling, colliding premonitions and snapped. The bedclothes heaved as he flung himself upon the weeping Inga. Their perspiring flesh locked together and the wild gyrations became a rhythmic, sensuous motion. A low sigh of contentment escaped Inga's open lips even if she realized that Lomas's actions were prompted more from hate than love.

Next morning Lomas and Andrei partook of an early breakfast, allowing the girls the luxury of extended dozing. After the meal Andrei brought his small Volga saloon around to the front of the house.

'Listen, Ilyich,' he said with earnest entreaty, 'if the police *are* looking for you, as Nina says, you'd better hide in the back. There's a couple of rugs and a load of flying gear to cover you. It's about 27 kilometres to Borispol and I'll go a back road I sometimes use.'

Lomas agreed wholeheartedly. All precautions, now that the flag was down, made sense.

Andrei gave the empty street a cursory inspection and opened the car door. Lomas lunged in, curled himself up on the floor and started piling rugs, flying helmets and an old leather coat over his body. Andrei gave the untidy pile a finishing touch and surveyed the result.

'Can you breathe?' he asked.

'Enough,' came the muffled response, 'but how are we going to do this tomorrow with two of us?'

'Now who's looking for difficulties? Let's see how this trip works before we start worrying about that. Anyway, I suppose I could make two journeys if it came to it.'

The city was barely awake and those citizens in evidence were scurrying to work. A slight mist hung in the cold air. Andrei drove rapidly in an eastward direction cutting across the main arteries with the confident ease of one who knew Kiev like the back of his hand. Clear of the lights near St Vladimir's, he raced for the Darnista Bridge, his eyes searching for signs of a traffic check. There was no avoiding the bridge and it was the one point that had him worried. But it was a needless worry. In a flash he was over and away. Out beyond Darnitsa, however, on the minor road that led to Gogolev before a branch double backed towards Borispol, a lone policeman with signal baton red-winked the car to a halt. Andrei knew the chap and smiled at him confidently.

'Playing cops and robbers today are we?'

The policeman glanced into his car, then

lost interest in his task.

'Some guy wanted for murder, but there's more to it than that.'

'How come?'

'They had us all out yesterday,. Searched a lot of houses in Kiev, put a block on the bridge, the lot. Acting on a tip-off, they say. It seems to me they're trying to crack a nut with a sledgehammer, murderer or no murderer. I think there's more to it than meets the eye.' The man pursed his lips and looked knowing as he imparted his tit-bit of opinion.

'Well, I'm going flying, whoever you're after,' said Andrei as he released the clutch.

'Don't blame you, Comrade Zenkevich, though it's hardly my tiffle. Aeroplanes turn my stomach.'

From his cramped position behind the two bucket seats Lomas listened to the exchange with more puzzlement than concern. Had not Nina insisted that the police had actually used his and Inga's names yesterday he would have been convinced that it was for someone else they were hunting. To have a dragnet out in Kiev 5000 miles from the scene of the crime – a crime which, even if proved, was no more than a local murder – just didn't make sense. A new line of thought came to him. Maybe Nina had just said what she did in an effort to get rid of them. Maybe the poor girl was frightened. He couldn't blame her. He could only hope her fright wouldn't lead her to do something silly.

He remained silent, waiting for Andrei to say anything there was to be said. The wheels bumped over the poor surface, each vibration transmitting itself to those parts of Lomas's body that hugged the floor, particularly the left thigh. He wondered why it was that car designers hadn't got around to removing the annoying hump between the front seats.

Half an hour passed before Andrei said, 'You okay? Only another two kilometres.'

Lomas tried to stretch and failed. Andrei felt the movement.

'Stay where you are. They've police on the gates. Borispol is lousy with 'em.'

'Hope they're no more enthusiastic than your pal down the road.'

'Don't worry, the gatehouse knows me. Now shut up till I say otherwise.'

Above the rattle of the car Lomas caught the roar of jet engines warming up. A gust of excitement caught him as he flicked his mind to aeroplanes. The inadequacy of his flying experience over the last decade began to swell to proportions bordering upon cold funk.

They were on smooth tarmac now. The hushed wheels allowed other noises to intrude. A heavy vehicle thudded by, going the other direction. Voices floated through the driving window to be drowned by the urgent scream of take-off as a giant TU hurled itself skywards. The movement of the car ceased. Another voice, louder than the jet, shouted near his car.

'Morning Comrade Zenkevich. Don't often see you on a weekday.'

'Got a couple of days off.' Andrei sounded relaxed.

The car moved forward again, gathering speed. It stopped again after what Lomas judged to be about a kilometre and reversed a few yards.

'You can surface now, Ilyich. No one's around.'

Lomas required no second bidding. Throwing off his assorted covering, he emerged on to the car seat and eagerly looked about him.

'Where are we?' he asked.

'Down the back end of the airport. Borispol is a bit of a mixture. It's home to *Aeroflot*,* the military and DAAF. Our section adjoins the MIGs so we're in good

* The Soviet airline.

170

company. I've backed up between these old hangars so that nobody can see you emerge. You'd better come in the front.'

Lomas climbed awkwardly over the passenger seat. His movements had become jerky and clumsy with nervousness.

'When we get to the tower let me do the talking,' Andrei continued. 'They already know about you. You're a friend of mine from Irkutsk I've not seen for a long time and are staying with me a few days. Your name's Boris Shepilov. Got that? Boris Shepilov. If you have to talk go back to the old days. Tell the truth about your life and flying. Don't try to be clever and bring things up to date. There's been so many changes you don't know about and they'll smell a rat.'

'What am I supposed to be?'

'An engineer. It'll cover a multitude of sins. Stick to one of your previous jobs in the West if you like.'

Lomas caught the drift of Andrei's thinking and nodded absently. He guessed his friend would be around to bale him out of any tight corners.

'Let's go,' he said, and Andrei let in the clutch.

The control tower was a large, squat cabin

with an upper storey of hexagonal panes of anti-glare glass. It adjoined a hutment of asbestos sheeting gleaming white in the weak sunshine forcing itself energetically through the mist. Beyond lay the flying apron, a vast expanse of grass dotted here and there with an aeroplane and a red and white striped landing beacon. A collection of half-derelict hutments, many with broken windows and doorless portals, stagnated on the edge of a field. Through the departing mists a double line of MIG 22s looking like regimented cockroaches stood before a complex of camouflaged buildings with high curved roofs. Still and silent, with hardly a movement around them, they offered an aura of deadliness magnified by the roar of the bigger, unseen, jets behind them.

'Do you get any interference from those things?' Lomas asked, his eyes still on the MIGs.

'Only on occasions such as an operational exercise, when they shut down DAAF flying altogether. All our calls emanating from our tower are of course monitored by theirs, so everybody's in the picture.'

'What about the civil jobs?'

'Again only on occasions like an emergency. It happens very seldom. We keep away from their flight paths though. Their radar's pretty hot and they get touchy if they think we're cramming them.'

They'd reached the door at the base of the control tower. Lomas felt the eyes of one of the duty staff upon him through the anti-glare above. The door flew upon him before Andrei could get his hand on the knob, and a cheerful youngster, tussle-haired and mildly handsome, emerged in a hurry.

'Hello, Andrei old son, fancy seeing you on a day of toil! Thought you were strictly a weekend bird. What'll the current five-year plan do without you... I know, I know' – he flashed gold-filled teeth over his shoulder as he departed in a breeze of flapping jacket and tie – 'You've demoted it to a six-year plan.'

Andrei smiled apologetically to Lomas.

'Our clown,' he explained. 'Never serious for a moment, even when he's flying. He'd have been chucked out long ago, but he's got ability. He can make an aeroplane do anything.'

A corridor, its fibreboard walls liberally sprinkled with notices, weather reports and political slogans, led them to a big, untidy room cluttered with canvas chairs and small collapsible tables. At one end a serving hatch

173

displayed two shelves of none-too-clean glasses surmounted by the inevitable portrait of Lenin. Half-a-dozen men lounged in the chairs smoking and reading magazines.

'The canteen,' announced Andrei, as if they had entered the Czar's banqueting hall. 'It's the place we hang around in while they put the machine together after the last chap's used it. Come and have some tea.'

Nobody took the slightest notice of the couple except one tubby individual who, slapping his copy of *Krokodil* down, sidled up to them. His little pig eyes flicked over Lomas.

'Ah, strangers in the camp,' he murmured with mock suspicion.

Andrei, with obvious reluctance, felt obliged to effect an introduction.

'Boris, this is Comrade Golovko. Comrade Golovko, Boris Shepilov.'

'Pleased to know you,' said Golovko with an insincerity bordering on rudeness.

'He's an old school friend of mine from the back of beyond; Irkutsk. Used to go flying together when we were hardly more than kids. Wants to be put through his paces. His wife and he are staying with us a couple of days.'

Golovko appeared neither satisfied nor

dissatisfied with these explanations. He nodded absently and moved away. A woman in a dirty white overall served them green tea in tumblers. Separately, she handed out wrapped sugar lumps.

Leaning against the counter, Andrei began a monologue on the pre-flight procedure adopted by pilots together with various rules and regulations insisted up by the authorities. Lomas listened in a vague, disinterested manner, his eyes upon the various aircraft he could see through the wide, uncurtained windows. Twice his attention was centred upon a sleek monoplane being refuelled from a pump at one corner of the concrete assembly apron.

'What's that little low-slung machine being tanked up?' he asked during a pause in the recital.

Andrei looked at his friend sharply, as if about to reprimand him for inattendance, but thought better of it.

'It's a little single-seater Sokol. Czech job and a nifty one. Most of 'em are two-seater, but this is a special for stunt flying.'

'What's its range?'

'The two-seaters can do upwards of 800 kilometres cruising. This one, with less weight, I suppose could put another 100 behind it, maybe more.'

Andrei thought he could see the reasoning behind Lomas's questions.

'Don't get ideas,' he added, dropping his tone. 'That Sokol's not for the likes of you or me. It's only in transit here. It goes off to Kuybyshev tomorrow for a trade fair.'

Lomas was not to be deterred.

'What's its speed?'

'Max about 400 km. As I said, it's a nifty job. The Czechs are better than us at the small machines. There were some four-seater Aero's here recently. Larger things, but they could still spin circles round our Jaks.'

Lomas appeared to lose interest and Andrei returned to the lesson. In a neighbouring room, empty, windowless and musty, one wall was entirely covered by a set of talc-covered maps giving a topographical picture of territory within a radius of some 300 miles of Borispol. Coloured pins dotted the area sparsely.

'Those are other bases. The yellow ones are DAAF like us; the red military or civil, and emergency landing zones only. You see DAAF have strips at Odessa, Sevastopol, Kishinev,' Andrei lowered his voice again. 'But remember what I said earlier about a restricted fuel intake at bases close to the

Black Sea.'

Lomas hadn't remembered. He'd been looking at the little Sokol job, weaving fantasies again.

'Repeat it,' he demanded.

A look of exasperation, eclipsed by a mirthless smile, crossed Andrei's face.

'At bases close to the State border they restrict your fuel intake. It's a precautionary measure, you understand. In theory one is allowed enough juice to reach the next DAAF base, where, if it's an inland one, you can fill up to your heart's content. In practice, they're not too fussy, but so much depends upon circumstances. If the duty officer knows you, if the fuel-issuing chaps like your face–' Andrei shrugged and spread out his hands. 'I've spoken to the man who will be on duty tomorrow at Odessa – he's all right – but you can never tell.'

Lomas nodded. He was taking it in this time. It was probably the moment when his latest fantasy began to crystallize into a decision.

A mock-up of the cockpit of a Jak occupied the two men a further hour and Lomas abruptly became a willing pupil. Funny how little had changed over the years. Bigger and faster and sleeker jets, yes, but the basics remained the same. The little club aero-planes were hardly different to those of 20 years ago; just a few refinements here, an improvement there. As Andrei droned on everything began to slip into place. Memories of his few solos in England and, further back, those post-war days when he and Andrei were enthusiastic amateurs rose to mind. Now Andrei was the expert. He had beaten him in the flying game, though for Lomas there were no regrets. His friend's knowledge was going to come in mighty useful.

A youngster in an unbuttoned flying jacket, a helmet dangling from his hand, entered.

'It's all yours, Andrei,' he announced in boyish tones. 'Tank half full. The compass has a tendency to stick, but a tap releases it. I've told the mechanics. You're on dual, aren't you?' He gave Lomas a friendly glance.

Andrei went through the rigmarole of the Boris Shepilov story.

Out on the field the little Jak stood ready. Before leaving the hutment Lomas and Andrei donned the leather jackets and helmets that they had taken from the car. It wasn't strictly necessary, Andrei had said, but it got cold aloft. Lomas scrambled into the little aeroplane beside Andrei and sat automatically checking the instruments as Andrei fastened the cockpit cover and went through the pre-take-off litany over the radio. Control said okay to go, adding runway designation and barometric pressure.

'Okay,' repeated Andrei, setting the altimeter. 'It's all yours.'

The engine fired at the first stroke. Lomas chalked up an alpha to the maintenance crew. He turned the machine into the wind and made an easy take-off.

As they gained height and Andrei ceased jabbering about throttling back and the other technicalities that had already come instinctively to his mind, Lomas understood anew the urge that drove man into the sky. A great peace blossomed around them as the flat land below became an upturned green sky. Clouds and air currents were the new elements of life, a clean, fresh life away from the petty absurdities of man's natural domain.

He watched Kiev, threaded like a conker upon a string that was the Dneiper, float beneath the port wing. Wisps of cloud broke the dark mass of the handsome city, giving it an ethereal quality that was but a mirage.

Somewhere down there was Inga. She was a mirage, too. Handsome but dangerous. What a mug he'd been to get himself mixed up with a woman, particularly an ambitious woman like her.

Yet there was a trace of sadness in his smile as, unseen by Andrei, he lifted a hand in silent farewell.

CHAPTER FIFTEEN

Anatoli Spassky was a great one for playing cat and mouse. Once his instinct told him the locality of his prey he was content to sit and watch outside the hole with feline patience. Not for him the paraphernalia of cheese baits and complicated ruses. A fugitive, however experienced, invariably made a mistake and gave his position or his intentions away. In this case the prey was not experienced. The couple had blundered their way across the USSR having the luck of the gods. Their giveaway was imply a matter of hours.

Colonel Spassky had moved up to the front line so to speak and was installed in a neat little office belonging to Kiev Criminal Police Headquarters. From his desk he had a view of the Khreshchetik, a pleasant change from the watery Amur. The bustle of its traffic and the movement along its sidewalks was a distraction he found most welcome during the waiting hours. It calmed and soothed his nerves which, to be honest, had taken a bashing over the last week or two. That the ignominy of dismissal and possibly worse had nearly been his lot had shaken him more than he cared to admit. And the threat still lay over him; hovering like a vulture.

This fact had already rattled his self-assurance to the extent of forcing him to instigate an evening search of certain areas of the city following what turned out to be a false tip-off. Everything had been highly inconvenienced, a lot of his men had exhibited themselves in the street, and the incident had started a flurry of rumours. It was all very untidy, unnecessary, and those above could well read into it blind panic. He was being more cautious now. The tip-off had to be from an impeachable source for subsequent action to be contemplated.

Spassky's policy of caution was put to the test the day following the fiasco of the search. The source of the new tip-off was KGB, but what made it more reliable was the fact of it coming through simply as a normal security report. The agent at the DAAF air strip at Borispol had put through a request for a precautionary check on a certain Boris Shepilov who, with his wife, was staying at the home of Andrei Zenkevich in Kiev. KGB headquarters had investigated. They could trace no Boris Shepilov answerable to the description given, but knew of Zenkevich. The description of Shepilov fitted Lomas. That was when the report was laid before Spassky.

If the wife turned out to be Inga Reprostovich, then he, Spassky, was home and dry. The address of the Zenkevich household lay before him on his desk. If either of them had the tape it was likely to be the girl, so he would go for her first. It wasn't necessary yet to stir up a hornet's nest at Borispol.

As he gave the order for the apprehension of 'Madame Shepilov' on the grounds of 'helping the police in the furtherance of their enquiries,' Anatoli Spassky took not the slightest notice of the buzzing of a small two-seater aircraft winging a path through a wisp of cloud above the edge of the city.

CHAPTER SIXTEEN

The little aircraft rocked erratically as it began the long glide into Borispol. Throttled back, the engine allowed the propeller to idle, and Lomas could feel the wind resisting the lowered flaps. The altimeter needle quivered and climbed slowly backwards round the clock.

Those two hours of flying had done more for him than he believed possible. It had restored a shaken confidence, a sense of indecision, not only in his ability to fly, but also in his determination to tackle the task ahead. The rudiments of flight, the little reflexes and stabilizing adjustments that he had once been laboriously taught and which had lain dormant in a closed compartment of his mind, were released to guide his handling of the machine. Andrei had carried out little in the way of instruction. There had been no need for it. Instead he had answered, to the best of his ability, the multitude of questions concerning air regulations, weather conditions and base security measures that Lomas had flung at him.

Only as they were approaching Borispol had Lomas produced his bombshell.

'Don't raise a load of reasons why it can't be done, Andrei, but I'm having that Sokol.'

Andrei was silent for a moment. He didn't even appear startled. Lomas thought he hadn't heard the statement.

'Did you hear what–'

'Yes, I heard,' Andrei came out of his reverie. 'I noted your interest earlier. No, it wouldn't be impossible, but you forget one thing.'

'What?'

'It's a single-seater. Even if you were able to get Inga into the cockpit with you its range would be correspondingly reduced and–'

'I'm going alone.'

This time Andrei was shocked. He stared at his friend in incredulous disbelief.

'How can you? Isn't that a pretty low sort of trick? Poor girl, you ask her to marry you, then go and ditch her at the last moment.'

'Poor girl my foot!' Lomas was stung into replying. 'She's had me on a string ever since I set eyes on her. Inga's nothing but an opportunist. It'll be she doing the ditching once I got her to the West.'

Lomas didn't much care what Andrei thought of him, but decided not to push the revulsion too far. After all, it could reach a point where another ditching could result. To have Andrei walk out on him at this juncture would be fatal. His tone softened as he pressed the explanations.

'No, I've been thinking about the matter for a considerable time. It's not a sudden decision. After all, the other thing notwithstanding, she's a Russian. She probably wouldn't be happy in another country and nothing very terrible will happen to her here. It's me they're after.'

'Why?'

Lomas saw he was skating on thin ice.

'Well, I'm the black sheep aren't I? I'm the one who's broken all the rules.'

'Ilyich, did you commit a crime back in Khabarovsk?'

Lomas glared ferociously back into the eyes that held his own.

'Don't be a damn fool, Andrei. Why should I want to murder anyone? They're using that as an excuse to hunt me down.'

Andrei appeared less convinced than before, but, with the runway in sight, his attention was diverted.

The ground lifted towards them. For a

moment Lomas thought he was taking it too fast and would overshoot. Then the wheels skimmed the ground, touched, bounced, and steadied. The grass, acting as a slow brake, hugged the little machine to a gradual halt. Pushing up the throttle, Lomas ran it confidently towards the sheds.

Climbing out of the cockpit on to the wing, he realized how cold it was. He'd been glad of Andrei's flying jacket. The sun had retreated under a counter-attack by a heavy concentration of grey cloud and the airport looked a depressing, colourless place in the monochrome of mid-afternoon. Even the big jets were still as he and Andrei walked stiffly towards the canteen.

In a small ante-room Andrei handed in the Jak's ignition key to an elderly man sitting on a stool. Lomas watched the custodian rise with a grunt and hang it on a rack containing some dozen others.

He nudged Andrei.

'Is the key for the Sokol there?' he whispered.

Andrei peered at the board, hesitated and addressed the old man.

'Josef, is the transit pilot around?'

Josef shook his head.

'No, he's been in town all day, Comrade

Zenkevich. His key's still in his machine so they can run it into the hangar overnight.'

The old man's whole life was tied up with ignition keys, their presence or otherwise forming a basis for conjecture on the whereabouts of their owners.

'Is anyone still out?'

Josef automatically glanced at the board.

'Comrade Tvardovsky is away another two days. There's just Comrade Kapitsa. He should be in anytime now.'

In the canteen they each had a large bowl of *borsch*. The room was empty save for the serving woman, and she was pottering about in a recess behind the counter.

Andrei gave his friend a wry smile.

'Had you been staying another night you could have stowed away a good meal before you left us. Nina was really going to show off her culinary expertise tonight. She'll be disappointed.'

'I'm sorry, too. A hearty breakfast for the condemned criminal and all that. I'll just have to make do with another *borsch*. By the way, what time do they lock up around here?'

'At dusk. Aircraft are locked up, as I told you, unless explicit instructions from individuals are received.'

'Were I to telephone control from outside, say I was Comrade What's his name of the Sokol, and that I had decided to set sail overnight instead of with the dawn, would there be any eyebrow raising?'

Andrei thought for a moment. Grudgingly he affirmed that he might get away with it.

'Where's the nearest telephone outside this building?'

'There's some in the terminal building at the airport.'

'Let's go then.'

Meekly Andrei allowed himself to be shepherded out to his car. He was disappointed in his friend. This unkind rejection of a girl with whom he'd involved himself was not like the Ilyich he once knew. They'd got into some scrapes together in the old days, but they'd never lost their honour. He felt tarnished, unclean. No longer was it a case of simply not wishing to mar his respectability. If it had to be marred it was important to him to know with what. The thing was beginning to stink. He'd let Ilyich make his confounded telephone call, drop him back at the base and get the hell out of it. How he was going to break the news to Inga he hadn't the faintest idea. Unlikely as it was she'd see it that way, but maybe she was well rid of her new boy friend. If that's what Western decadence did to people, maybe the Soviet Union wasn't such a bad place after all.

Uneasy and self-conscious, Andrei led Lomas through the bustle of the airport reception hall to a line of telephone kiosks. Strident announcements crackled through the Tannoy infecting the crowd with a tangible nervousness that showed on every face. He passed Lomas a *copek*, told him what to say and moved away. The nervousness was infectious.

CHAPTER SEVENTEEN

The apprehension of Inga Reprostovich took place without incident. She was taken completely by surprise and surrendered without fuss to the three-man patrol that carried out the duty. A brief search had unearthed the Marchenko tape from amongst her few effects. The apprehending officer had reported that the girl seemed to have no idea as to its significance.

Colonel Spassky had interviewed her alone in his office. He used the soft approach, emphasizing his own very personal friendship with the girl's father. He commiserated with her on the sad loss and the subsequent bout of madness that had led her into the spot of bother she was now. But this business, he went on, occasioned obviously by her grief, might be quietly overlooked if he used his full and very considerable influence. He was careful not to make his words sound like a threat or even an inducement, hoping that one kind act by him would trigger an offer by the other.

Inga had remained silent, staring at the floor. She appeared to be in a state of shock reinforced by a bout of deep depression. Anatoli Spassky gazed at her in tolerant admiration. He couldn't really blame any man for running off with a girl like that. She was quite a woman even if he was seeing her under circumstances of considerable strain. And the strain suited her, he decided. The brown eyes cast down, the determined tilt of her jaw, the shapely mouth clamped shut in brave rejection. He appreciated that. He hadn't realized Igor's daughter had such talents. His eyes rested on her body, tasting it as one does a good wine. The breasts were heaving slightly above a slim waist and, from where he sat, Spassky could see the beginnings of a promising thigh.

'You know, I might be able to help your friend, too,' he murmured, following a long interval during which the noise of traffic had intruded with abrupt clarity. Spassky was in an expansive mood sugared with relief. He could afford to be tolerant.

Still Inga made no response; her expression remained unchanged. She didn't seem to have heard.

Spassky sat back in his chair and fiddled with a pencil.

'We're picking up your friend when he returns from the airport. I thought it would save him the embarrassment of a more public apprehension,' he explained gently, not mentioning that a squad of men had been despatched to Borispol to ensure that he got no wind of what was in store.

He tried a new tack.

'Inga – you don't mind an old friend of your father's calling you Inga do you? – you don't know how he – your father – was drowned, do you?'

Inga raised her head and spoke for the first time.

'It was an accident.' Her words were faint, parrot-like but defiant.

'What would you say if I told you that we have reason to believe his drowning was not an accident?'

'I should say you were lying.'

Colonel Spassky transferred his gaze to the window. Outside the grey afternoon was in that stage of indecision between dusk and evening. Most of the traffic had its side lights on.

'We think the Englishman Lomas murdered him.'

If Spassky thought his announcement would jog the girl into some kind of reaction he was disappointed. Her eyes were back on the floor.

'Why should he?' she said without great interest.

'I don't know, but I might want to find out. It is my duty you know. On the other hand, if you can persuade me that it was an accident, I would have no cause to hold him.'

'Would you let us both go?'

'Of course.'

There was a tiny inflection of interest in Inga's voice as she put the second question.

'Would you be able to help us get married? It would mean my emigrating to England.'

'I would do what I could. Naturally I can't promise anything definite. But you are a Jewess. It should not be impossible.' He shrugged expansively, raising both hands off the desk.

'How does one prove such a thing didn't happen when I wasn't even there?' The hopelessness began to return to Inga's voice.

'Tell me in detail about the visit to Khabarovsk of your English friend. Right from the moment you set eyes on him. Tell me your first impressions, what you especially noticed about–'

The telephone's strident tone intervened.

Spassky said 'Yes' into the receiver, projecting his annoyance into the syllable. He listened to the spasm of words and the frown on his face gave way to startlement.

'You mean he's gone on his own!'

The instrument made confirmatory noises and Spassky slammed down the receiver.

'Your good English friend has ditched you,' he growled with heavy sarcasm before reaching again for the telephone.

For a full five minutes he busied himself issuing curt instructions, giving terse descriptions, to the duty officers of a number of airforce and DAAF bases. He used his KGB status to cut short the red tape, aware that he was exceeding his authority. That side of the business had been cleared up with recovery of the tape. The rest was actually a criminal job. But Anatoli Spassky was a tidy-minded man. He liked his cases neatly terminated and labelled 'finis'.

The last call made, he swept the telephone away towards the edge of the desk and transferred his attention once more to the girl. Another shock awaited him.

Inga was half out of her chair, her whole body quivering. But it was her face that held him. He was seeing what Lomas saw in St Sophia, only the malevolence was deeper.

Again the mask had descended upon her features so that it exuded an aura of un-diluted hate. The eyes smouldered beneath half-closed lids and her small hands were balled into tight fists.

'Inga,' he began, more out of concern for her than the furtherance of his duty. 'Are you all right? Can I–'

'Comrade Colonel,' replied the girl in a toneless voice, 'I think I can help you with what you want. I think I can prove to you that Lomas murdered my father.'

CHAPTER EIGHTEEN

The telephone call from Borispol had gone down a treat. Following Andrei's directions, Lomas had spoken his piece through a handkerchief wrapped around the mouthpiece, and the duty officer the other end had accepted his every request and instruction with a murmur. Yes, he would have his machine ready for immediate take-off. Yes, the tanks were already full. He quite understood the Comrade Major's desire to reach Kuybyshev that night. He would be pleased to warn Kuybyshev control of the change of flight plan. Probably the handkerchief bit was a bit melodramatic. As a transit pilot they'd hardly know his voice anyway. But it was part of the game. Lomas was beginning to enjoy himself.

So he was a major, was he? He mustn't forget that. Little lapses could lead to big disasters. Not that much could go wrong now, surely? His new-found flying ability had given him great confidence. He could see little that could stop him.

Andrei had driven him to within sight of the base and dropped him off. He'd walk the rest of the way so as not to arrive too soon after the telephone call. In less than half an hour it would be dusk; dark enough to hide his credentials, light enough to set him on the way.

His goodbyes to Andrei had been perfunctory. The relationship had soured since his declaration of going it alone. A bit old-fashioned was Andrei, but he'd get over it. So would Inga. No doubt the fur would fly for a time, but she'd soon find another man. A pity in a way about Inga. A striking woman like that could do something to his ego back in Britain. A case, perhaps, of lost opportunity there, but assuredly a narrow escape, too. As well as paradise Inga was equally capable of making life hell.

There was hardly a soul in evidence at the base. He carefully dodged old Josef, who might have recognized him, donned Andrei's flying jacket, and carefully buttoned the flaps of the helmet before striding out purposefully towards the little Sokol almost hidden in the gathering gloom.

A mechanic came out of the hangar to meet him. He was a boyish youth, eager to please. Lomas nodded at him and turned his head away. He had no idea whether the transit pilot was short or tall, fat or thin. This was a contingency not covered by the plot; a moment where simple luck held the cards.

'All ready to go, Comrade,' vouchsafed the younger man.

Lomas raised his arm in silent acknowledgement and increased speed to reach the aircraft just ahead of him. Once in the cockpit stature would matter little.

The cockpit cover was closed and of a type new to Lomas. To show his ignorance would be fatal, yet how the hell was he to get in? Little gusts of panic blew cold in his stomach as his eyes searched wildly for the release. Within the moment of hesitation the mechanic drew level, jumped up on to the trailing edge of the wing and the cockpit yawned open. As Lomas likewise mounted the wing the two faced each other for no more than a fraction of a second. Yet, in that fleeting instant of time, Lomas saw the tiny change of expression that preceded bafflement, a slow-motion switch of emotions as willing servitude gave way to surprised bewilderment. But the implications were given no chance to register. Even before he was properly settled in the pilot's seat Lomas had started on the run through of pre-take-off preliminaries. Turn on master switch, ditto fuel tap, note gauges operating, test control column, wind trim wheel to fullest extent. Okay. Fuel, brakes, ignition, on. Now press starter button and pray.

A choking snarl and the engine shattered into life. Lomas watched the mechanic back away from the wing, his overalls fluttering in the slipstream. The turmoil seemed to have successfully blown any dangerous suspicions out of the chap's head. Damn him, once airborne the little bugger could think what he liked. Lomas throttled back to 1000 r.p.m. and transferred his gaze to the instruments as they began to flicker information. The artificial horizon levelled off, the gyroscopic direction indicator steadied to give a single compass heading, oil pressure at 60, brakes off, power on. With a jerk the machine moved forward to bump like a wounded moth across the rough turf. Nothing much anyone could do to stop him now, but better if he could get through the niceties.

Reluctantly he braked, allowing the tail to lift expectantly off the ground, as he gave the engine another burst of full throttle. The grass lay flat in sullen abeyance. Throttling back again to an idling 700, he switched the radio to 'transmit' and, against the hiss of

202

the propeller, said, 'GKN to tower. Permission to take off.' A metallic voice in his ear granted it, adding the usual pre-take-off instructions and a bonus of local weather conditions. Lomas switched off, opened the throttle, mouthed a triumphant obscenity into the 'dead' microphone, and, as the Sokol gathered speed over the smoother grass, he eased it confidently into the air.

Levelling out, he turned the aircraft's nose north-east on a course of 270° magnetic in the general direction of Kuybyshev with lights on so that the tower would get the right idea. After a quarter of an hour he went down to 500 feet, switched off his lights and turned south. His battered map, supported by a flight plan from Andrei, he spread like napkins over his knees.

Below, little nests of lights winked at him from a few scattered homesteads. The dreary countryside had slid from view, the black earth of the great Ukrainian plains finally hidden by a universal darkness of equal intensity. For Lomas the night was a friend, it confounded his pursuers and cloaked him from their view. Somewhere back in Kiev they would still be searching for him, clumsily setting up road-checks and dragging the suburbs. And here he was flying like a bird; winging his way back to his own world of sanity and normality. He didn't think Inga would shop him. At least not right away. Certainly Andrei wouldn't, nor even Nina. But given a couple of hours' start they could put it out on Moscow Radio if they liked. By then he'd be approaching the Black Sea and there was little they could do about it. Yes, he'd been lucky, incredibly and superbly lucky.

Perhaps it could be considered only a pity therefore that the real transit pilot had chosen to ring the base minutes after Lomas's departure.

Lomas had been flying due south for a little over an hour with the engine throttled back. He was sacrificing speed for fuel economy since fuel was going to be another element of chance where perhaps his new-found optimism might just conceivably have miscalculated. He resisted the urge to pile on the knots and held back his speed to around the 200 mark. That way he would make the Turkish coastline with juice to spare. And maybe he'd need every drop he could save. Andrei was right with his remark about the hazards of a landing in the nearest Turkish territory. Lomas eyed the folded map and noted with unease the ominous expanse of dark brown, a turbulent sea of rock, that was his chosen sanctuary. Only at the very edges of the coast there showed a thin sheen of green to calm nerves that were beginning to fray the veneered edge of his confidence.

The lights of a fair-sized town showed up beneath the port wing. Balta, he supposed. That or Pervomaisk. From the air towns by night always confused him. The spread of illumination invariably gave an impression of a larger town than it was. He remembered an occasion in an airliner when he had mistaken little Minden, in Germany, for Hanover. Funny how tiny specks of unimportant memory got jogged to the fore by an occurrence of only slight similarity. Balta, or Pervomaisk, he would reach the Black Sea coast in half an hour. His intention was to pass well to the west of Odessa. He could hardly avoid the radar scanners as he approached the coast, but over the chief Black Sea port of the Soviet he'd be asking for trouble. They'd have a multitude of gadgets around the city. No, he'd set a course for the Dniester Gulf some 40 kilometres to the west. He'd start losing height in another ten minutes and, if he was lucky, he'd pick up the line of the river at Tiraspol and could follow it to the gulf. Of course it might be too dark, but he didn't think so. Things always looked blacker at 600 feet than they were at 250, which was the altitude to which he intended coming down to confuse the radar. There was always a possibility of missing Tiraspol and the Dniester. Well, if so, there was no need to sweat. Another landmark, further west, was the lake complex around Sasic. He'd be hardly likely to miss that. West of Sasic and he'd be intruding into Romanian air space and he didn't think they'd like that. Romanians and Russians were not the greatest of friends beneath the surface and there had been stories of unpleasant incidents. No, he must avoid Romanian territory at all costs.

How quiet everything was! Even the engine had settled down to a contented purr. Down below a new darkness had taken over from the splash of light that was Balta or Pervomaisk. Odd how one's ears became attuned to continuous noise. Little wisps of cloud flicked the wing-tips lighting up the fabric and, in some strange way, illuminating the registration markings in an eery glow. A slight turbulence bucked the aircraft and, at the same time, changing the tempo of the engine to a spasmodic growl. Lomas watched his instruments. Everything was going fine. Fuel consumption just beginning to show. Height still 600. He'd bring that down in a minute. Revs 2100 r.p.m. Just right. That growl again. But the turbulence had passed? And it didn't seem to come from the engine. Sounded for all the world like a jet. Could he have blundered into a civil air corridor? More likely just his ears playing tricks. Lomas grinned to himself, conscious of his own nervousness, but glanced over his shoulder just the same. The velvet darkness was all he could see, an inky patch that should have comforted him but didn't.

Any second now the lights of Tiraspol should appear up front. He didn't think he'd ever have occasion to welcome the lights of a Soviet town, but this one would be an exception. It could confirm his position and, at the same time, offer an illusion of companionship. Lights meant people; even if only Ruski people, but people all the same. He couldn't remember ever having felt so lonely on a night flight.

Yes, there it was dead ahead. The glow in the darkness matched that of the sense of achievement that warmly suffused his heart. Doubts that had begun nagging him were flung aside by the violence of sudden excitement. He was content to ignore the fresh growl that impinged upon his ears until it abruptly became a matter of new concern.

What the hell was it? The doubts started flowing back again and he felt the thudding of a heart that threatened to work loose from its bearings. He searched the darkness, his eyes raking the black velvet until red spots were dancing with fiendish glee. The noise grew to a banshee scream.

Lomas never saw the silvery shape that rocketed up from behind until it drew level close to the starboard wing. One moment it was there, the next it had gone in a great surge of sound. For a moment he thought he was imagining things, his overwrought mind conjuring up fantasies. Almost in slow motion the answer burrowed out of the cotton wool of his brain.

MIGs! A cold hand gripped his bowels, twisting them into taut spirals. Sweat broke out on his forehead to lie like a wet carpet against a brain that refused to function. 'Get down to the deck you bloody fool,' said a voice that he only gradually recognized as his own. Even as he sat rigidly digesting this information another scream welled up from behind.

With the scream came something else. Above the fearsome racket of the jet engines there arose a great blast of sound to smash the air in a hideous crescendo. Lomas's senses reeled as fright burst out of the fear in his guts. He vomited a thin stream of saliva down the front of his flying jacket.

Machine guns? Surely not? For God's sake, no. They wouldn't, not without a warning. It would be bestial, inhuman.

In front of Lomas's face the left-hand portion of the instrument panel dissolved into a mash of broken glass and woodwork. The compass, the rev counter, the fuel gauge disappeared. A crunch of bullets bit deep into the fabric of the fuselage.

'Dive, you idiot, dive,' Lomas heard his own scream, and, this time, reacted. He pushed the column forward and, on full throttle, threw the machine earthward. As he went he caught a glimpse of another silvery shape hurtle by, trailing fire from its exhausts.

The needle of the altimeter quivered and fell back. Lomas watched mesmerized as it sunk to 500, 400, 300. Just above the 200 he pulled out. He was aware of the ground now, a darker shadow against the night.

The lights of Tiraspol had swollen to a flood of brilliance. Over to the far left a glow infused the sky. Odessa. It could only be Odessa. At least he was still on course. The ground gave way to a glass-like substance and because lights twinkled beyond it took a full ten seconds to register the fact he was flying over water. Another ten and the realization came that the water was the Dniester Gulf. In a matter of minutes the friendly lights below would be extinguished by the cold, dark emptiness of the Black Sea.

Lomas throttled back the bucking Sokol to a more economic speed. To end up fuelless in the middle of the drink would be as lethal as those MIGs. And a lot slower. He scooped a sprinkling of broken glass out of his lap and surveyed the panel. Except for the three instruments, no great damage appeared to have been done. Nothing visible at any rate. With the fuel indicator gone he wouldn't know about the tank. A nervous spasm momentarily shook him as he imagined precious liquid streaming from a fracture.

Around him all was quiet again. As long as he hugged the ground he'd be quite safe from interception. Fast pursuit aircraft would never dare to go much below 500 feet. With no lights showing they'd probably lost him anyway. At that level ground-to-air missiles and radar too would be the more confused. In spite of the fresh surge of relief and complacency, Lomas searched the dark skies for sign of his pursuers, listening for the dreaded scream of their approach. He watched the ground, too, with a marked lack of confidence in his altimeter. Thank God, he mused, for the Nogaisk Steppe; the dead flat territory he had chosen for a springboard of escape.

No more lights littered the ground. Cautiously descending to 150 feet, Lomas perceived the ruffled surface of the open sea; a myriad frothy 'sea horses' leaping playfully as a fresh wind galvanized them into action. It was the first warning of a new menace.

Hardly had the land receded when he felt the cross-wind. It buffeted the aircraft, pulling it off-course and disturbing his sense of direction each time he made what he hoped to be a corresponding navigational adjustment. Without a compass, he had no idea as to how far off-course he was being blown and within half an hour it was simply a faith in his own judgement that held back a new panic. The gusts were blowing north-west across his path and, although by no means of gale force, he judged them severe enough to maintain corrective measures. His sights were on a slice of green territory in front of the Turkish town of Adaparzari, some fifty miles east of Istanbul. There would be perfection, but a hundred miles on either side would suffice. The scope was wide, the odds against error comforting.

He began to contemplate his movements upon landing. He would take all care possible not to smash up the aeroplane, of course, if only for the very good reason that by doing so he would save smashing up himself. He would then find the nearest village, but if it was too dark perhaps it would be wiser to remain in the machine until daylight. No doubt a policeman would be found eventually who would put him in touch with the relevant authorities. The delicious prospects unrolled to sustain and warm him like a heady wine.

A violent gust threw the nose of the machine sideways and Lomas felt the tug of the control column. He compensated as best he could with a flick of the rudder and watched the nose swing back. A solitary light below drew his eye as a ship scythed through the breakers. Lomas tried to plot its likely course, but there were too many possibilities. Istanbul, Varna, Constanta, Odessa, Sevastopol, Kerch, Novorossilsk, Sansum, Inebolu. There were dozens of ports. The Black Sea was a Piccadilly Circus of shipping routes. Maybe it was a Turkish boat on its way to a

Turkish port. Maybe it wasn't. As far as he could judge it was sailing due west, which was odd. His map showed most of the shipping lines as running in the general direction north and south. But, hell, that didn't mean anything.

His calmer nerves allowed him to speculate a moment upon Inga. He wondered what she would be doing. She would know by now, of course. Perhaps he had been a little unkind to her, but she was a menace. How much did she know? Maybe it was just inspired guesswork, but it could be equally damning. It would foul up their future together. No, better the clean break.

The engine gave a polite little cough, eclipsing Lomas's contemplations beneath a brick wall of fear. A moment later it had recovered itself and was running as smoothly as ever. A speck of dirt in the carburettor, the fuel line or something without doubt, he told himself, but blood showed where he was biting his lip.

Another half-hour and he could expect to see the lights of Turkey. He'd better start gaining height soon if he didn't want to ram a mountain. A few of the inland peaks rose to 6000 feet and though he'd no intention of flying deep into the interior, he didn't know how abruptly the coastal ranges started. Perhaps, when he neared the coast, it would be an idea to change direction and fly alongside it for a time. Sort of inspect the lie of the land so to speak. But he mustn't forget the fuel; there couldn't be–

Another cough, a double one, as if it were trying to clear its throat, came from the engine. At the same moment lights showed up ahead. Lomas's eyes riveted themselves upon them desperately probing for recognition. They weren't ships, that was for certain. Too many of them, and, thank God, look, there were more behind. It could only be a town. Land, wonderful land, was only five minutes ahead. Of course, he'd miscalculated. He'd been flying flat out when he'd crossed the Soviet coast and so had gained time. Lomas started whispering platitudes to the engine, willing it to carry on another few minutes. At the same time he slowly surreptitiously, increased altitude in preparation for an emergency glide. The notion of coming down into the drink appalled him. So near and yet… He must make it, he *must*.

At 400 feet he straightened out. He strained to catch a fleeting glimpse of a landmark that would spell the name of the town as it materialized from a glow into a city of some size. If the place was as big as it looked and was not another illusion it could only be Istanbul. He tried to pick out a minaret; then, remembering its geography, searched wildly for the Bosphorus, a sight of a distant sea of Marmara and an indication of the hills on which the city stood. His mind flew back across the years to his schoolday geography lessons. The seven hills of Istanbul, the Bosphorus ferries. Damn it, what else did he know about this former capital of the Turks? Geography had never been a favourite subject.

Suddenly his eyes caught on to a landmark that did mean something. A straight line of lights shouted 'airport'. It must be Istanbul. No other Turkish city within range could boast such an amenity.

The engine coughed again. Lights rose up to meet him and Lomas pulled back on the column to avoid a hill. Well, that fitted anyway. Thank God something did. An idea came to him. Dare he transmit and ask for permission to land? What would be the Turkish reception 'drill' for a defecting pilot? He'd heard ugly rumours concerning the return of Russian escapees on the Armenian border. But that was different. Down there was a land border and events were governed by local authorities of mixed sympathies. No, Istanbul would be another matter. He switched on the radio, but no comforting crackle scoured his ears. Damn, the thing must have stopped a slug. He'd have to go in without permission. The airport people would love him, but they'd have to lump it.

He came down low, made a pass at the runway and soared into the sky. Nobody seemed to take the slightest notice. A bunch of people beside a vehicle on the edge of the runway looked up at him but didn't show undue excitement. Lomas circled the perimeter and came in again. This time was for real. He wasn't trusting enough for another look-see. The juice in the tank must be lower than the sweat on the brow of a gnat. The landing lights bored in on him, escorting him to the tarmac. He was pleased with the touch-down. It made a sort of signature to his epic of escape.

The jeep he'd seen earlier started moving towards him. Lomas pushed up the throttle and trickled forward to meet it. He'd have a bit of explaining to do, no doubt. They met within sight of the control tower. Lomas tipped back the canopy, levered himself stiffly out of the cockpit and turned to meet the bevy of uniformed men. One of them, who appeared to be in charge, stepped out of the group. He spoke quietly in carefully pronounced English.

'We meet at last Mr Lomas,' said Colonel Spassky. 'Welcome to Sevastopol.'

CHAPTER NINETEEN

The trial of Lomas – *née* Ilyich Palatnik – has passed into legal history. Britain made a loud noise with her extradition attempts, but these foundered upon the proven case of murder. Yet that crime was hardly mentioned at the special investigation held in the sealed wing of Kiev prison that belonged to the Ukrainian KGB. For two months he was kept there in solitary confinement while being interrogated by a team of KGB investigators who eventually entered a charge of high treason against him.

Early in the New Year the case came before the Supreme Court of the Soviet Socialist Republic of the Ukraine. It was a closed court and most of the proceedings took place *in camera*. Lomas's original defection from Soviet-occupied Porkkala was highlighted by the prosecution though the main charge was the stealing of the Marchenko tape and his probable knowledge of its contents. On this charge a willing witness was Inga Reprostovich. There was one break in the proceedings when the court was thrown open for the benefit of the Western press, who were becoming restive. This was when the criminal police were able to have their say about the murder of Igor Reprostovich. Again his daughter was able to give a creditable performance against the defendant.

Lomas's lawyer attended both courts and pleaded his client's case most eloquently. In the criminal court he made an impassioned plea for mercy on the grounds of the motivating power of revenge. In the KGB court he argued that there were no grounds for a conviction of treason. Whether either plea helped is a matter of conjecture, but at least Lomas escaped a death-sentence. Instead he got twenty-two years' imprisonment and corrective confinement.

When it was all over Lomas was allowed to see Inga. She was a picture of radiance, her face lit by her biggest smile ever. She entered his cell with dainty steps, taking care to make minimum contact with the prison furnishings. Lomas rose as if to kiss her, thought better of it and sank down again at the small table.

Inga seated herself opposite, brushed imaginary dust from her beige dress, and, with mock tragedy, shook her head.

'We are an unlucky couple, aren't we?' she said brightly. 'I lose my chance to come with you to England, you lose your way in an aeroplane.' She stopped talking suddenly as if she had just thought of something. 'You know, Lomas, you shouldn't have done that, you shouldn't have run off like that. Girls don't take kindly to being jilted, you know.'

Lomas looked at the floor. He wasn't quite sure if she was taunting him or not. He started to mumble some apologies.

'Oh, it's no good crying over spilt milk,' continued Inga. 'All is not lost. I'm free at last from my father. Life won't be bad now. Even my pride won't be too hurt. After all, if I want it, I've got you as mine for the next twenty-two years, haven't I, Lomas? You know, it was only an afterthought that made me pick up Father's tape. I thought it might turn out to be useful.'

Lomas detected a whimsical note in the silken voice. And that smile. It always did floor him.

This Large Print Book, for people
who cannot read normal print,
is published under the auspices of

THE ULVERSCROFT FOUNDATION

... we hope you have enjoyed this book.
Please think for a moment about those
who have worse eyesight than you ...
and are unable to even read or enjoy
Large Print without great difficulty.

You can help them by sending a
donation, large or small, to:

**The Ulverscroft Foundation,
1, The Green, Bradgate Road,
Anstey, Leicestershire, LE7 7FU,
England.**
or request a copy of our brochure for
more details.

The Foundation will use all donations
to assist those people who are visually
impaired and need special attention
with medical research, diagnosis
and treatment.

Thank you very much for your help.